SECOND BEST SISTER

Carol Stanley

AN
APPLE
PAPERBACK

SCHOLASTIC INC.
New York Toronto London Auckland Sydney

For Jean V. Naggar

ISBN 0-590-40052-5

12 11 10 9 8 7 6 5 4 3 2 1   8 9/8 0 1 2 3/9

Printed in the U.S.A.   01

First Scholastic printing, May 1988

I don't want to exaggerate here. . . .

I can tell my parents don't have much of an idea of who I am, and have pretty much given up making a big parent-daughter connection with me. I don't want to exaggerate here. I'm not saying they let me walk around in rags and tatters and forget my name or anything. But I think you could definitely say I'm their kid, and Julie's the light of their life.

Look for these and other Apple Paperbacks
in your local bookstores!

With You and Without You
by Ann M. Martin

Last One Home
by Mary Pope Osborne

Hurricane Elaine
by Johanna Hurwitz

Just a Little Bit Lost
by Laurel Trivelpiece

Miracle at Clement's Pond
by Patricia Pendergraft

Fifteen At Last
by Candice F. Ransom

Chapter 1

The first thing I do every morning is make myself breakfast — generally a Tab and a microwave cheeseburger. While the cheeseburger is getting waved, I go get the newspaper off the front porch, bring it into the kitchen, open it up, and read the comics page.

Not all the comics. I'm actually pretty selective. I never read any of the serious ones, and only the best of the funny ones. And I almost never read the stupid puzzle at the bottom of the page — it's called PUZZL'R. It's pretty much aimed at seven-year-olds. At fourteen, there are quite a few things I'm way beyond.

This morning, though, my eye was just sort of magnetized to the PUZZL'R. It was one of those drawings with the headline: WHAT'S WRONG WITH THIS PIC-TURE? In the drawing, there was a house and a tree and a lake, and a lot of other smaller stuff — a dog and a squirrel and some flowers. And all of this was regular-looking. But then up in the clouds, there was an upside-down cow, which was supposed to be what was wrong with the picture.

It was an incredibly dumb puzzle, but I found myself staring at it for the longest time. What I was thinking was — I'm the cow. In my family, it's me — Meg Swenson — *I'm* what's wrong with the picture.

Everything else around here fits right in. My mom and dad, for instance. They're really happy down here in Florida. They're into fixing up this old house they bought when we moved down to Marlin Beach. They both like their jobs. And, even after being married for about a million years, they still crack up at each other's jokes and never ever fight.

My sister Julie also fits right into the picture. Actually, the picture was kind of drawn around her. It's because of her that we moved down to Marlin Beach in the first place — so she could go to Surfcrest Academy, which is this expensive private school with an incredibly mediocre academic program. The thing is, it has the best swim coaching in the country. My sister Julie is a honcho swimmer, what the sports magazines call "an Olympic hopeful."

I was still looking at the PUZZL'R picture when Julie came downstairs, late for school as usual.

"Hey," she said. It's what she says instead of saying "hi" like a normal person. She picked it up at Surfcrest. They all say jock things like that and give each other these incredibly athletic handshakes and backslaps all the time. It would make you sick to hang out there for longer than about three minutes, believe me.

"You want to go to the show with me tonight?" I asked Julie. I had to shout the question because she was running the blender. Her breakfast is this health shake goop made with fruit and milk and protein powder and multivitamins. She made me take a sip once and I just about gagged, but I guess this is the kind of jump start your body needs if you're going to make it through a day of hand-shaking and back-slapping and majorly dumb and jock-y conversation. Not to mention the swimming. Everybody at Surfcrest swims.

"What?!" my sister shouted back at me over the blender, this industrial-strength model my parents got her. It's about as loud as your basic steel foundry. I don't know how my parents sleep through it every morning, but they do. My mom teaches girls' phys ed over at Marlin Beach

High School, and doesn't have classes until eleven. Dad has his own business and doesn't open up until noon. They both sleep in mornings, and Julie and I have to fend for ourselves in terms of breakfast and finding clean socks and getting ourselves off to school on time.

"YOU WANT TO GO TO THE SHOW TONIGHT?!" I started to scream even louder. Julie — to be helpful — shut the blender off in the middle of what I was saying, so that I wound up screaming — "SHOW TONIGHT?!" in this bloodcurdling way, over a background of total silence. We both had to laugh. And then Julie smiled and said, "Sure."

One of the best things about my sister is that she'll almost always say okay to doing stuff with me. She never asks first who's in the movie, or why I want her to drive us out to the ocean at dawn. She just says "sure." Like it's a good enough deal just doing something with me, and what the something *is* really isn't important. I haven't quite figured out whether this is because she's such a great sister, or because to a person who spends about five hours of every day swimming back and forth in a rectangle of chlorinated water, anything else seems like amazing fun.

"Check you later," she said now. "I'm

late as the Mad Hatter." She grabbed her health shake, to drink in her car on the way to school. It was seven-twenty-eight. Julie has a pre-class workout and so has to be at Surfcrest by seven-thirty. I still had twelve minutes to drink tea and read the comics, eight minutes to dress, and ten minutes to walk the four blocks over to Coconut Palm Junior High, where I am in my last days as an eighth-grader.

Coconut Palm, in my opinion, is about the stupidest name ever given to a junior high school. When I write to my friends back in Minneapolis, I duck around actually telling them the name. I just say "my school" or "the junior high." And I *never* mention that the football team is called the Coconuts.

Joey was waiting for me, as usual, on the front steps of the school. He was wearing a camouflage T-shirt and olive drab shorts. Joey is usually dressed as though he's going to be rushing into war at any moment. Which is odd, given that he doesn't believe in war, or even in playground fights. The other guys know this and so never pick on him — not even the real bullies like Steve Keller. It's just too humiliating for them to stand there taking jabs at a short, skinny kid with thick glasses who's never going to hit back.

Joey is my best friend at school. My only friend, actually. This lack of other friends is completely my fault. I just messed up my chances here right off the bat. People always say it's hard to transfer schools, but I think the truth is that in most places the kids have been talking to each other since kindergarten and are getting pretty bored, and are glad to see a little new blood show up. Just being from someplace else makes you interesting — for a little while at least. If I'd been the least bit friendly in those first weeks, I probably could have been pretty popular down here, like I was back in Minneapolis.

But I was furious at my folks for transplanting me, as if I were some potted begonia. I just had to prove to them and everybody else that I was absolutely miserable here. I stuck to my surly and silent program straight through the time when I could have been making friends. If some kid came up to me during those first days and asked me what snow felt like, or if you could keep snowballs in your freezer until summer, or how I was liking it at Coconut Palm, I'd just act surly and silent, and pretty soon everybody left me alone.

Except for Joey, who really *is* surly and silent. When he spotted me in algebra class, he thought he'd found a fellow soul in this sunny, cheery place where he feels totally lost.

"So, what's happening?" Joey said to me as we went into school together. This is just a manner of speaking. Nothing ever happens to either of us.

"I hate the end of the year," I told him. "Everything's due at once. I was up until two doing my report on 'Paraguay, Land of Contrasts.' I made a collage/product map." I showed him.

"What's this?" he asked, pointing to one of the baggies I'd stapled to the map part.

"It's supposed to be cotton, one of Paraguay's big exports. It's really some acrylic yarn from a sweater my mom's knitting. This is a terrible project. Maybe my worst ever. My quebracho wood is really pencil shavings. My yerba maté is supposed to be some South American herb drink, but where am I going to get that? So I just emptied a Lipton tea bag. Half these pictures aren't really of Paraguay. This farm field is Argentina. The beach is in California. Do you think Forbert will find me out and mark me down?"

"Nah," Joey said. "He's grading so many stupid reports this week, you could probably slip a Vermont maple grove in there and get away with it. I'll meet you at the door after school. We can go out to the cove."

"Okay," I said and started off toward Elmquist's classroom. Then I remembered, and turned around and called back to him. "I forgot. I've got some good news!"

And I wasn't kidding. I really did.

Chapter 2

The day seemed to take *forever* to get to three o'clock. Partly this was because I didn't have geography until fifth period, and so I had to carry my Paraguay project around with me almost all day. It was too big to fit in my locker. Carrying around a huge collage/product map of Paraguay is one of those things you can get away with doing only if you are one of the very coolest kids in school. Then suddenly everyone thinks Paraguay is the most fascinating country in the world and weren't you cool for figuring that out. But I'm not considered very cool at all, and so everyone just smirked as I lugged my project around from class to class. I guess they'd thought ahead, and made their own projects small enough to fit into their lockers.

"Paraguay, si?" Ron Mussman said to me, smirking.

"Neat baggies," said Jill Percival, who was walking with Ron.

The whole day was more or less like this. I was late to Elmquist's class — only by seconds, but with her that's still practically grounds to call out the firing squad. I think junior high teaching might not be the best career for Elmquist. It seems to make her extremely tense. She gave papers back and I got a C-minus on mine. It was on *Little Women*. I knew it was a sloppy job, but I'd been hoping she wouldn't notice and would give me a B on it. I can really kid myself sometimes.

All in all, it was a pretty stupid day. And so I was glad to see Joey waiting for me on the school steps at the end of it. We could go hang out at the cove and I'd tell him the good news.

Joey and I found the cove by accident one day last winter. We'd been exploring along the deserted beach outside town and were talking about something and kept walking farther than we ever had before. Finally we got stopped by this huge sand dune. At least it was enough to stop me. Climbing sand dunes is, as far as I'm concerned, about as much fun as having your tonsils out. But Joey bounded ahead and reached down to give me a hand up.

"Come on, lazybones," he taunted. "Even

you can make it over this eentsy-weentsy baby dune."

"Eentsy-weentsy?!" I wailed, but let him drag me up the side of it anyway. I should say that I'm probably the least athletic, most out-of-shape fourteen-year-old in the world. I expect some important team of doctors from some big research institute to come to my house any day now and verify this. Give me a certificate.

Finally — when I had about two pounds of sand in each of my tennis shoes and was just about to sit down and refuse to go one inch farther — we got to the top of the dune and looked down. It was pretty amazing, I must say. It looked like those photos from travel ads for vacations on unspoiled islands. The beach was ultra-white sand, the water turquoise. And even from as high up as we were, you could see all the way to the bottom. You could also see that the water in the cove was filled with fish of about a million colors. Wrapping around the cove were dunes as high as the one we were standing on. Anyone who wanted to get there would have to go through a bit of trouble.

"Oh, no!" I moaned, being a person who likes to go to as little trouble as possible. "Now we have to go all the way *down* the side of this dune!"

"Yes," Joey said patiently. "But the beauty of dunes is that although you have to climb up them, you get to *roll* down."

"Oh, I couldn't do that!" I protested. I hated to even do a somersault on a flat floor in gym class. "Impossible. I'll just walk down real slowly."

"You'll do no such thing," Joey said in this surprising leader-of-the-safari voice. "Dune-rolling is one of the world's great experiences. I'm not going to let you pass it up just because you're a little timid." He put a hand on my shoulder and looked me hard in the eyes and said, "Trust me, Meg."

I nodded. "Okay," I said.

"I'll go first. Wait until I'm maybe ten feet down and then follow. Put your arms over your head and push off."

I did what he said. At first it wasn't too scary. But then I picked up momentum and was suddenly rolling downhill at what seemed like about two hundred miles per hour. It was like being on a roller coaster, only with no little car holding you inside. And so from there on, I did what any person with my high levels of courage and bravery would do — shut my eyes and screamed all the way to the bottom.

Only when I'd stopped rolling did I open my eyes again. I sat up and looked around.

"Wow," I said, kind of breathing the

word out more than saying it. "This is the most beautiful place on earth."

I still think it's the most beautiful place, even though I've rolled down that dune onto that beach maybe fifty times by now. Actually, I just keep thinking it's more and more beautiful as Joey and I keep discovering new things about it. Like the fish and the seagulls.

Joey saved up and bought a snorkel, a mask, and fins so he could float around in the cove's waters and look at the fish. He says there's a reef out a ways that's sort of a fish disco — it's where all the fish hang out.

Sometimes he floats for an hour or so like that while I sit on the beach and draw in my sketchbook. I would like to see the fish, but I really can't. I kind of have this policy. I don't go in the water except to take showers. It's a small matter of principle. Everything in my family revolves around swimming, and so I want to stay out of that.

Sometimes, on weekends, Joey and I bring lunch and stay the whole day. Other times we just slip over to the cove for an hour or so after school — especially when we have something important to talk about.

He and I are not the only people who know about the cove. There's also Adelaide, who calls it "Adelaide's Cove." She showed up one of the first times we were there. Joey was off snorkeling and I was lying on my back, watching the gulls looping down from the sky and then back up again, when all of a sudden there at the top of the dune was this old lady with a cane and a small, moplike dog.

"Yoohoo!" she shouted and waved at me like crazy. Then she began this quick little sidestep down the dune, with the dog scampering around her, barking at her feet. It was a pretty amazing sight. Adelaide is quite old and heavy and about six feet tall. That first day she was wearing these huge old full-sail Bermuda shorts from the fifties and the loudest Hawaiian shirt I'd ever seen. She is not your typical old person.

When she got to the bottom, she said, "Wellwellwell, I see you've found my beach."

For a second I thought maybe she meant she owned it, that I was sitting around on her property. But then I realized that someone dressed as thrift-shoppy as she was was probably not the owner of expensive beachfront property. She introduced herself and her dog, Sweetie, who was no breed you could put your finger on.

"I came to feed my friends," she said, opening up an old grocery bag she was holding and pulling from it huge handfuls of torn-up bread, which she scattered all around us on the beach. Suddenly, all the gulls, who had been sort of aimlessly diving and soaring, gathered together like a cloud and descended around us to pick up the bread in their beaks and then flew off again.

Adelaide doesn't seem to mind sharing the cove with us, which is big of her, since she found it first.

I was glad she wasn't there today, though, since I wanted to talk with Joey alone. He started pressuring me right away for my news, while he was still peeling off his school clothes, getting down to the swimsuit he had on underneath.

"So? What's the big story?"

I held onto my news a little longer, just to drive him crazy. I pulled a candy bar out of my pocket. It was pretty squooshed from getting rolled on all the way down the dune, but Joey still took the half I offered him.

"So?" he said again.

"Mrmrph mffmp . . ." I started to say.

"Maybe if you waited until your mouth wasn't quite so full of chocolate, I might be able to actually understand you."

I swallowed and then started again.

"I *said* that my dad has managed to snag us a couple of part-time jobs for the summer."

"At Jungle Rapids?" he asked.

I guess I should explain that — unlike other kids' fathers who sell insurance, or do carpentry like Joey's dad, or just go to some office every day where you don't really know what they do — my dad dresses up every day in a pith helmet and khaki shorts and shirt and goes over to run the Jungle Rapids ride he has out by the highway. You've probably seen the billboards if you've ever been driving through this part of Florida. Bwana Dave's Jungle Rapids. My dad is Bwana Dave. It's one of the three most embarrassing things about my life. On this list, it's right between the stupid, satin-strap retainer I have to wear at night on my braces, and the fact that my real name is Margaret.

Anyway, Jungle Rapids is basically a fake mountain with fake waterfalls and fake jungle trees and bushes, and winding down around the mountain is this rushing stream. People pay perfectly good money to sit on little plastic mats and shoot down this stream, get scared to death, and wind up soaking wet. Sometimes when I don't have too much else to do, I hang around the fence at the bottom and watch girls who came with dates and got all dressed up and fixed their hair perfectly and put on an hour's worth of makeup. It's fun watching these girls come off the rapids.

But our jobs were not going to be at my dad's place. We were supposed to work next door, at the Mr. Bozo Miniature Golf Course. I told Joey.

"Oh, that's great," he said. "I thought you were going to say we had jobs at your father's embarrassing ride, but this is so much better — breaking into the dignified and fast-growing field of miniature golf. These are executive positions, no doubt. We'll be reporting directly to Mr. B., I assume?"

"Joey," I said. "Come on. You know we're incredibly lucky to get any summer jobs at all. And this should be really easy stuff. We just have to hand out the balls and putters and keep people moving smoothly through the course. Think of it as a kind of public relations job. We'll be representatives of the Mr. Bozo spirit."

Joey rolled his eyes upward and fell back onto the sand to show me how stupid he thought the job was. I knew he was happy to have it, though. Summer jobs around here are tough to get. Until my dad came up with these, through his friend Steve Edmunds — Mr. Bozo — Joey didn't have anything lined up, and I was going to have to spend the summer baby-sitting for the McMahan kids, who look like four ordinary brothers and sisters, but once you've baby-sat for them you know better.

"Well. All right. I guess," Joey said, drawing the words out, as if he was giving the job his most carefully considered consideration.

"Give me a break, Joey," I said, picking up my sketchbook.

"Okay, okay," he said, pulling on his flippers.

Okay what?" I said.

"Okay, I'm tremendously grateful to Bwana Dave for getting us these jobs."

"Good," I said a little huffily, to put him in his place. As he flapped off toward the water, I added, "I'll tell you about the costumes later."

He kept walking until he got to the waterline. At first I thought he hadn't heard me and then he turned, eyes wide, and shaped his mouth silently into the word, "Costumes?!"

Chapter 3

Joey and I kind of got lost in our own private worlds at the cove — me sketching, him floating around watching the fish. I was late getting home. My mom and Julie were already fixing dinner. I could smell it through the screen door as soon as I hit the front porch. Stir-fried something with green onions.

I should probably mention here that my family is not Chinese. Otherwise you might get that impression, given what we eat most of the time. I suspect we eat more Oriental food than most Oriental families around here. Once I even asked Hillary Chung what they ate for dinner at her house. She just shrugged and said, "I don't know. Same as anybody else — pizza, burgers. Sometimes my mom makes lasagna."

She should stop by our house sometime, rediscover her roots. On almost any given night, she'd find my mother and Julie gathered around the old wok stirring and frying and sizzling and steaming. The thing is that Oriental food is lean and full of protein and low in fat and all that — all the stuff my sister needs for her swimmer's diet.

"Hi, everybody! I'm home!" I shouted as I came in. If anyone asked where I'd been, I'd just say studying in the school library — my basic, all-purpose excuse. My family doesn't know about the cove. It wouldn't be a secret anymore if I told them. It wouldn't be as special a place. Adelaide agrees with us on this. We have a pact with her. If we ever run into each other — on the street or something — we pretend we don't know her and she pretends she doesn't know us. Otherwise, people would want to know where we all know each other from.

"Hi, honey!" my mom shouted out to me now, as if she was happy I was home. But by the time I got into the kitchen, her concentration was back on the wok. Julie was tossing in the various chopped-up ingredients while my mother stirred like crazy.

"There's plenty for you, too," my mom said, as they were scooping the dinner from the wok onto a big platter.

"Uh," I said cautiously, "just what is it tonight?"

"Tofu," my mother said, turning and

holding the platter out to me. I can't even look at tofu, much less eat it. So, "Nofu," I said, opened the freezer door, pulled out a frozen enchilada dinner, took it out of the package, and popped it in the microwave.

"You'll be the first kid in Marlin Beach with rickets and scurvy," my mother said. "It'll be pretty embarrassing for the family. They'll come with a minicam and interview us. They'll run a little identifying tag under me saying 'negligent mother.' "

I tried to imagine this and knew no one would believe my mom could be negligent. She's a person who just radiates niceness and efficiency. Both she and my dad are from Swedish farm families and have blond hair and freckles and cornflower-blue eyes. They look like they met each other in the church choir, which they did. I look a lot like them, only my hair is even blonder — almost white really, and I'm already taller than my mother. They think I might wind up as tall as my dad.

Julie looks nothing like us. She's slender and dark with high cheekbones and eyes so brown they're almost black, like her hair. You see, my sister's adopted. When my folks were first married, they wanted a baby, but my mother couldn't get pregnant. And so they adopted Julie, who was a year or so old already. Then, about two minutes after they got her, my mother got pregnant with me.

The other funny thing that happened is that, although I'm their natural kid and look like them and all, Julie is really much more their spiritual daughter. Nobody mentions this, but it seems astonishingly true to me. She's athletic like they are and shares their easy good nature. I, on the other hand, am about as athletic as your average ninety-year-old and am a crabby, sarcastic person.

I can tell my parents don't have much of an idea of who I am, and have pretty much given up making a big parent-daughter connection with me. I don't want to exaggerate here. I'm not saying they let me walk around in rags and tatters and forget my name or anything. But I think you could definitely say I'm their kid, and Julie's the light of their life. Which, you would think, would make me insanely jealous of my sister. But Julie is an impossible person to have any sort of bad feeling toward. She's just too nice.

"How'd your Paraguay project go over?" she asked me, as she pulled up a stool and set her plate and chopsticks down on the counter bar where we eat most of the time.

"Oh, okay, I guess." Actually, Forbert spotted the pencil shavings right off the bat. Then he said the whole project looked "a little tired." I didn't want to sound like a whiner and so I didn't explain that I'd had to carry it around with me all day, knocking the corners up and loosening a couple of the baggies.

"Well, I thought it looked great," Julie said. "Very professional."

Sometimes I love my sister so much I just want to rush over and hug her. "Professional." As if there's a profession for the making of Paraguay projects.

"Are you still going to the show with me?" I asked her as the microwave pinged to show that my enchilada dinner was done. She nodded her head while taking a bite of tofu.

"Of course. What's on?"

"Something new with Charlie Sheen," I said.

"*So* cute," my sister said. "The boy is so very cute. What's the show time? I've got to crash early. Ian's putting us through extra sets tomorrow at *six*, if you can believe it." Ian Braithwaite is this Australian guy who's the honcho coach over at Surfcrest. My sister lives more by Ian's rules than my parents'. Actually, she doesn't really need rules. Mostly she's either in school or the pool, or too exhausted from both to get into any regular teenage trouble.

"I'll go call the theater," I said.

Julie drove us out to the CineQuad in the mall. I wanted to get some popcorn before we went in. Julie had a packet of dried fruit with her and didn't want to stand in the line with me and so just went on in ahead.

I almost didn't find her. She was down in front, on the left where we always sit. But I was looking for one person and she was two. That is, she and Brad Hunter were two people sitting side by side, extremely close together. *Quite* a surprise.

Brad Hunter is about the baddest guy in Marlin Beach. Which isn't really saying much. It's a pretty dinky town, and it doesn't take a lot to get a heavy rep here. All Brad really does, to earn this rep, is wear an earring and have his hair cut into a little tail in the back and ride a motorcycle. He also looks kind of like a younger Mel Gibson.

What I'm saying is that, although the guy is pretty cool, it's not in a way I'd think my sister would go for. I didn't even know she knew Brad — I mean, to talk to. Everyone knows who he is, because of the motorcycle and all. And so I was pretty surprised to see him sitting in the seat next to her. It wasn't as though the theater was crowded or anything. I mean, there were plenty of other empty seats.

"Look who I ran into," Julie said, when I got to their row. "Our neighbor, Brad Hunter." I thought that was stretching it a bit. Brad lives a couple of streets over from us. It's not like he stops by every week or so to borrow a cup of sugar.

"Hi," I said in my surly voice. I really have this perfected. It's pretty effective. It's the voice I used to drive away almost everyone at my school.

"Yeah, we just ran into each other and Brad said he'd sit with us," Julie rattled on in this weird, ultracheery voice, completely unlike how she usually talks.

"Great," I said in my most witheringly sarcastic voice, and plopped down next to her with my tub of buttered popcorn. I was pretty hurt, I'll admit. I thought this was going to be just me and my sister tonight — not me and my sister and this small-town hood. I noticed Brad was even working on a *Miami Vice* sort of stubbly look, but he's only seventeen and doesn't really have enough of a beard to pull it off.

The lights went down and the movie came on right after that, so I didn't get a chance to use any of my great sarcastic comments on him. To be honest, I didn't really think of any of these great comments until about half an hour into the movie. Basically, I think of almost all my great comments about half an hour after I could have used them.

The movie was pretty good, I guess, but I couldn't really concentrate. Especially after Brad took my sister's hand and she let him hold it throughout the whole rest of the movie. I couldn't believe it. I mean, I thought Julie and I were really close. I don't tell her every little thing that happens to me, but a boyfriend isn't exactly a little thing. If I had a boyfriend, I would definitely let Julie know right away. Plus, I thought Julie already *had* a boyfriend, or a sort of boyfriend — Tom Bauser, who swims butterfly on the Surfcrest boys' team.

Of course, there was still an outside chance that Brad wasn't Julie's boyfriend, that she really had just run into him here tonight, and that she was just too nice and didn't want to hurt his feelings by asking him to let go of her hand.

This idea pretty much flew out the window after the movie, when we walked out of the theater, into the mall. Brad asked if we wanted to go to the Ice Cream Cottage for a sundae.

"Can't," Julie said. "Remember, I told you. Ian's got us doing early sets tomorrow." Apparently she knew Brad well enough to keep him filled in on her schedule. Because he's such a neighbor, I guess. I also guess neighbors kiss each other good-night in the mall — on the lips — because that's what Brad and Julie did.

I didn't say anything to her as we walked through the parking lot to her car. I figured she was the one with the explaining to do.

"I didn't know he was going to show up here," she said, finally. "He came by school this afternoon and wanted to go out to-night, and I told him I was going to the show with you. I guess he just wanted to surprise me. And then once he was there in the theater, what was I going to say? 'Please sit on the other side — this is an experience I want to share with my sister.'"

I could see she had a point.

"How come you didn't tell me this was going on?" I asked her.

She just shrugged as we got into the car. When she'd started it up and we were on the highway back into town, she said, "It's all happened pretty fast. He used to go with Marilyn Sanders and so he'd always be around the recreation room at Surfcrest. And then they broke up and he came by one day and wanted to give me a ride home. I told him I had a car and he said he'd give me a ride home and then another ride back to my car. That was a couple of weeks ago. I've been seeing him since, but I don't know . . . I mean, I can't imagine Mom and Dad are going to be happy about this. And then there's the Tom problem. I guess I've been pretty chickenhearted about telling anyone."

I didn't say anything. We just drove through the night, next to the ocean, which you could hear underneath the sound of the car engine.

"You were going to be the first person I told," Julie said. "Honest."

I believed her and felt everything go back to normal between us.

"He *really* looks like Mel Gibson," I told her.

I was already asleep later that night when Julie came into my room, crouched down by the side of my bed, and shook my shoulder to wake me up.

"Hunh?" I said.

"Shhh. I don't want Mom and Dad to hear."

I nodded.

"Don't tell them about Brad and me, okay?"

I nodded again.

"I'll tell them eventually — if it gets serious. I don't want to rile them all up if this isn't going to amount to anything anyway."

I nodded understandingly.

Julie pulled my sheet up and tucked it around my shoulders in this sweet, motherly way, and said, "It was good having this talk with you."

I nodded again, even though it occurred to me that this "talk" was pretty much one-sided. Julie really could've had it with my phone machine. If I had a phone machine. But I did like that she was confiding in me. Plus, I kind of liked getting tucked in. My mother is big on me being more independent and mature, and hasn't tucked me in since I was about seven and woke up screaming in the middle of the night after having seen this really stupid vampire movie called *I Bite Your Neck*. I wondered what she'd do now if I started screaming. Probably she'd come in and talk to me in this mature, independent way about my nightmare. I *could* sort of imagine her tucking Julie in, though.

Chapter 4

The next week was the last week of classes, and it crawled by so slowly I began to understand the mental state of maximum security prisoners. I even checked off each day on the little teddy bear calendar I have pasted inside the front cover of my loose-leaf binder.

Finally Friday came, and it was a pretty good day — well, as good as a school day can be. Lunch was a big picnic out on the school lawn and then we didn't even have the last two class periods. Instead, we had a final dress rehearsal for the end-of-school pageant that night.

This year, the pageant — which is always a comedy — was called "Space Vacation." It was this sci-fi story of some kids from Coconut Palm who mistakenly climb aboard a spaceship and fall asleep. When they wake up, they're traveling through outer space, stopping at different planets in the galaxy. Every kid in school had a part in the pageant. Talented kids who could sing or dance or play instruments had bigger parts. The others were sort of wedged into the background.

I was in this big musical number about a third of the way through the program where the boy and girl land on a planet that's all ice. Some pretty funny stuff happens to them. I was in a sort of supporting role. To be exact, I was a dancing icicle.

There were twenty of us dancing icicles and all we did was sort of shuffle back and forth across the stage by the glacier backdrop, while the real singing and dancing was going on in front of us. I was covered head to toe in aluminum foil, so no one could even see who I was. But still, I was excited that my parents were coming to see me in this. I don't think they know I can dance at all and we icicles looked pretty good. Everyone said so.

The dress rehearsal was neat. Everyone was in a good mood, on account of school being over and all. Plus everybody was in costume, which in this weird way let everyone just relax and be normal. All the cliques and groups got broken down. For once it didn't matter if you were a gorgeous cheerleader or a fat kid, a basketball star or a nerd. For today you were an icicle or an amphibious bird or an uggie (creatures

from the planet Ug). Joey was an uggie —
and not happy about how stupid he thought
he looked in his uggie suit — and so I
hardly got to talk with him the whole afternoon. Who I *did* talk with was Jill Percival.
She is ordinarily so snobby that she doesn't
even bother snubbing someone as un-
popular as I am. But since we were both
icicles and had to wait forever until our
part of the show came up, she sat with me
and asked how awful it was having to wear
braces. She was going to get them over the
summer. She was just like a regular person
once you put her in aluminum foil.

And then her boyfriend, the ultracool
Ron Mussman, came over and teased us
about our "metallic look" and stuff like
that. It was pretty funny, I'll have to
admit.

I was on a roll of feeling good when I got
home. I was thinking maybe the whole
family could go out to the Seahorse Grill
for dinner before the pageant, to celebrate
my finishing eighth grade, which seemed
like something of an accomplishment. And
I figured that if I was going to get a cele-
bration, it had better be before my parents
saw my grades.

I'd really let them slide this year. I used
to be a B-plus student, but then one time I
overheard Mom and Dad consoling Julie on

her Cs and they were saying grades weren't all that important. Cs were perfectly respectable. And so I thought, why should I knock myself out trying so hard if nobody cared anyway?

I shouted around the house — "Anyone home?" — but no one was back yet. I supposed my folks were still at work, and I knew Julie had a big practice since Surfcrest had a meet the next day with its archrival, Boca Verde. I looked at my watch. It was only four-thirty.

I went in and took a fast shower. Ironically, being an icicle is hot work. Aluminum foil doesn't let your skin breathe and I was feeling pretty drenched. When I got out, I came into the kitchen, took some ice cream out of the freezer, and started to scoop it into a bowl. Then I saw that it was that ice cream substitute made out of tofu. I scooped it back into the carton and made a peanut-butter-and-jelly sandwich. You have to be incredibly careful around my house or you'll wind up eating something way healthier than what you're looking for.

I took my sandwich and a glass of milk upstairs to my room, which is really the attic of this old house my parents found us down here. This room is the only thing about my life here that's better than my life was in Minnesota. It really is great, though. One huge room with skylights in the middle and windows at either end to let the sea breezes rush through.

I keep it pretty stark-looking. I guess I'm an abnormal teenager in this way. I don't have my walls plastered with a million pictures of Michael J. Fox, or horses. I don't have a stuffed animal collection. I just have a bed with a pale blue spread, and a rug that's pale blue and peach and sort of Navaho-looking, except that we got it at Sears, so I doubt if it's direct from the reservation. It's pretty sharp, though. I also have a white dresser, very plain. And a white laminate drawing table under one of the skylights. This is where I do my drawing.

I draw a lot. I've been at it since I was really little. I think maybe I'm getting pretty good. I can now do complicated drawings without too much sweat. But I don't have any outside opinions on them because I never show them to anyone. They just seem too private a part of me. And so my parents have never seen them, or Julie. Not even Joey. I've been thinking lately, though, of showing them to Ms. Jenkins, my art teacher over at Coconut Palm, who thinks the stuff I do in her class is real good.

A lot of the drawings are of this imaginary land I've made up, which is populated by unicorns and butterflies and magicians. It's hard to explain, and a little embarrassing. I mean, what if I show this stuff to Jenkins and she starts laughing? What if it turns out that my imaginary world is incredibly corny and I just can't see it? When I think about it that way, it seems like the best idea is to just keep my drawings to myself.

The drawing I was working on was really all drawn. I was coloring it in now, and had that about half done. I sat down with my colored pencils and began to work. Coloring really absorbs my whole attention. I lose touch with the outside world completely. And so, when the phone rang a while later, I jumped about three feet in the air, sat there stunned for a second, then realized it was the phone and ran down to the second floor hall to pick it up.

It was my mom.

"Hey," she said against a lot of background noise. Why, I thought, is my mother saying "hey"?

"Where are you?" I asked.

"Over at Surfcrest." That explained it. The whole Surfcrest way of talking and acting is contagious. Like a minor disease. Even I can catch it. Once after coming back from one of Julie's meets, I slapped Joey on the back and said, "All *right*!"

"What are you doing there?" I asked my mother. I looked at my watch and saw that I'd been drawing for quite a while. It was a quarter after six. There was no way we could go to dinner and still make the pageant by eight. I had to be over at school by seven-thirty to get wrapped in my foil again. Oh, well. I guessed that she was calling to tell me they'd just meet me over at Coconut Palm later. Which would be okay, except the dinner would've been fun.

"Well, you know Julie's got a big meet tomorrow."

"Yeah."

"She's been having trouble with her open turn. Ian wants to give her an intensive coaching session on it, and your dad and I think we should be here. She's been practicing so long today that she's getting discouraged. We took her out for a quick dinner just now and she's resting. I think us being here will help her morale. Ian thinks that with the intensive, she can shave maybe two tenths of a second off her time."

"Great," I said. "So when's this intensive over?"

"Oh, let's see," my mother said. "I don't think Ian's going to be back until eight or so. So probably around ten. So you can fix yourself something to eat, can't you?"

"Sure," I told her. "I'll be fine. No problem," I said as sarcastically as I could. As I hung up, I wondered if they'd just forgotten the pageant, or if they'd never really heard me all the times I've told them about it. My brain felt funny, like all the circuits inside were melting down.

Then I went on a rampage through the house. First I dumped three bags of super-granola on the floor and shuffled around in it like a tap dancer gone berserk. Then I went into the family room and pulled all the cushions and pillows off the furniture and threw them all around the room. I could hear myself making this strange growling noise as I went. I sounded like a bear coming out of hibernation. I slid open the glass door in the family room and ran out into the backyard. I looked around for some havoc to wreak, but all I could see were my mother's few pitiful poinsettia plants, and they were already so scraggly in the heat that I didn't have the heart to yank them out of the ground.

So I just dropped to the ground and sprawled there in the path of the sprinkler, cooling off. I closed my eyes until all my anger at my parents and jealousy of Julie subsided from a boil to a simmer. I started out hating them all and wondering if I could join up with a circus and leave my family behind. Then I spun out into this fantasy that if I did that, they wouldn't even notice that I'd gone. Years from now, my dad would look up at my mother and say, "Isn't it about time that Meg was graduating from college?" And my mother would slap her forehead and say, "Meg! Where has she been all these years? Julie, go look up in the attic."

From there I shifted into this totally morbid fantasy where I got killed on the job at the circus — stomped by an elephant I was training. And then they were all so sorry. "We should've gone to that pageant," my mother told my dad in this one.

Eventually, when it was starting to get dark, I got up off the grass and went inside. I wrapped myself up in a blanket to ward off the air-conditioning. I went into the den and flipped on the TV. I just looked at whatever came on for the next few hours. I wasn't really watching any of it. When the phone rang and rang and rang about nine-thirty, I figured it was Joey, wondering where I was. I'd call him tomorrow. As for the pageant, I figured no one would really notice if there were twenty icicles or nineteen. Who cares about a stupid pageant anyway?

About ten, I started straightening things and sweeping up all the signs of my rampage. Then I went up to the attic and sat in the dark, watching out of my window until the three of them came home. They had a big pizza box with them and were all laughing as they got out of the car.

"Hey, Meg!" Julie called out. "Come on. Pizza time!"

I just sat very still and didn't answer, so they would think I was asleep. In a weird way, it was sort of interesting to sit there watching them without them being able to see me.

`Chapter 5

Saturday morning, I woke up still furious with my parents. I stomped around getting up and getting myself ready — slammed a few doors, rattled drawers in the kitchen, and ran the garbage disposal even though there was nothing in it. Just for good measure. And for double good measure, I turned the radio up about three quarters of the way on the hard rock station. This was a good example of my wimpy nature. I mean, anyone throwing a really decent tantrum would turn the radio up *all* the way. Me, I always chicken out — steaming inside, but only able to let part of it show.

I guess I was too scared I'd get yelled at by my mom and dad, and that they'd like me even less than they already did.

Skipping the swim meet would have made a good, silent statement, but I couldn't do that either. On account of

Julie. The night before hadn't been her fault. I might've mentioned the pageant to her, but I don't think I ever told her exactly when it was.

And this morning, she was close to a major freak-out of her own. As I was blowing my hair dry in front of the mirror over my dresser, I could smell chlorine and knew she had come up into the room.

"Can you talk to me a little?" she asked in this nervous, wimpy way. It's easy to tell when Julie's stressed-out. She hardly says anything, just kind of hops around and hums. It's like she's got all this surplus energy and has to burn it off somehow.

"Sure," I said, shutting off my dryer. "How's the old turn coming?"

"Turn, shmurn," Julie said disgustedly. "That's just not going to make enough of a difference. Mom and Dad and Ian have talked themselves into believing I can beat Irene Hofstadter. There's just no way. *No way.* Irene is like lightning through the water, an electric current."

"She must be a shocking person, then," I said with an absolutely straight face. And so it took Julie an extra second or two before a smile cracked through the gloom on her face, and she reached over and mussed up my hair.

"You make the absolute worst jokes,"

she teased me. "Why do I laugh at them? How can I laugh at *anything* right now? When I am about to be slaughtered by Irene Hofstadter, the Ace of Boca Verde?"

"Just give it your best shot," I told her. "Then if you lose, you can honestly say to yourself, 'That was the best I could do and that's that.' "

"Oh, Meg," she said, flopping onto my bed, "don't you see, in swimming, there's always something more you could've done. Extra practices. Better playing on your strengths or against your opponent's weaknesses. The possibilities are endless. The only way you've ever done enough is if you *win*."

The meet was at Surfcrest, which only has about three books in its library, but has two giant pools on its grounds — one for swimming, another for diving. There were a couple hundred people around the swimming pool — friends and family of both teams. Julie went off to the locker room and I headed up the bleachers with my folks.

Both my parents are jocks. My dad was on the track team in both high school and college, and still runs every day. My mother played basketball, and her college team made it to the regionals one year. She has a little plaque. Neither of them was ever the athlete Julie is, though. Hardly anyone is. Julie's in the top one percent or so. The stratosphere.

My parents saw right away that she had big potential. If Julie had been adopted by another family — say some musical family — they probably would've been giving her piano lessons and missing the whole point. Mom and Dad, though, put her right on the fast track. She had her first swim lesson when she was two years old, and Mom and Dad were right there at the edge of the pool. They've been there ever since. So in a way, every time Julie's in a meet, they're hanging onto her as she cuts through the water. The tips of their fingers touch the tile wall at the finish. They win or lose along with her.

Not me. I mean, I'm always happy for my sister when she wins and sad for her when she doesn't. But it's not as if she's swimming to rescue a capsized boatload of little kids. This is not life and death stuff. We are only talking about a sport here.

No one else around me this morning took this philosophical view. There was so much nervousness in the stands, you could practically see it hanging around in the air, vaporizing off the worried parents, like steam.

"How did she seem to you?" my mom was asking my dad now.

"A little tense, but highly motivated. Geared up. Did she sleep well?"

My mother nodded.

"Eight-and-a-half hours. And she did high-protein and megavitamins for breakfast. I made sure she shaved her legs."

I should tell you here — because otherwise you'd never guess this — that when it comes to these meets, everyone goes berserk trying to cut fractions of seconds off their times. They get down to astonishingly fine points, including shaving their legs — even the guys — to minimize the drag caused by hair. Sometimes I just want to say, Give me a break.

The girls in the first event — one-hundred-meter freestyle — were up on the starting blocks now, and the hubbubby atmosphere around the pool quieted down to one huge, held breath. And then the starter's pistol went off. Six girls leaped into the water in hard, smacking racing dives, and the place went wild.

Julie was in two events — the two-hundred-meter individual medley, and the one-hundred-meter butterfly. Butterfly is her stroke. If you've never seen it, it's just powering your way through the water — pulling yourself out of it, then throwing yourself back into it. If you've ever tried doing it, you know it's the hardest way to get from one end of a pool to the other. My sister makes it look like a breeze, though.

The Surfcrest girls took the individual medley, but mostly because Lucy Brent is the fastest high school girl freestyler in the country. The other three girls — doing breaststroke, butterfly, and backstroke — could practically have floated across the pool on rafts, drinking Cokes and getting a tan, as long as Lucy was in the fourth spot to finish the medley.

Julie's own time in the medley was a few seconds slower than Irene Hofstadter's, which sent my folks into the pits of despair. They barely saw any of the events between this one and Julie's hundred-meter fly. At one point, my dad looked over at me as if I'd just shown up. He gave my cheek a little pinch.

"You've got to go over and talk with Steve about those summer jobs," my dad said. "As soon as school's over."

"It is," I told him. "Yesterday was the last day." I said this in my most punky, sarcastic voice. I was hoping to trigger his memory about the pageant and get him to apologize. In my instant fantasy, he was crying a little at how sorry he was.

"It was? Oh. Well, then you and Jimmy should go over there this weekend."

"Joey."

"Right," he said distractedly. Julie had just come off the bench and was standing next to her starting block, pushing her hair up into her latex bathing cap. Irene Hofstadter had the lane next to her. An alarming thing about Irene was how much taller than Julie she was. It just seemed that wherever they were going, that six-inch difference would give Irene an edge in getting there first.

"Swimmers and timers ready!" the starter called out.

All six girls — three from Surfcrest, three from Boca Verde — got up onto their starting blocks.

"On your marks!"

They crouched down, on the platforms, arms behind them, heads ducked. Their concentration was so intense you could almost feel it coming off them in waves.

"Bang!" The pistol went off and along with it, the six girls. Quickly, they formed a V, like migrating ducks. Irene and Julie were the tip of the V, with the other girls in the side lanes fanning back behind them. By the time they were in the last length, it was impossible to see whether my sister or Irene was in the lead. They were *that* close. From where I sat, it looked like they slapped the edge of the pool at the exact same moment.

46

Everyone stood up and cheered. The Boca Verde fans were acting like Irene had won, and everyone from Marlin Beach was assuming that my sister was the winner. Then it came over the loudspeaker that the race was so close, it would have to be called by playing back the videotape. Everyone waited.

Finally, after what seemed like an hour, but was probably only a few minutes, they announced the judges' decision.

"One-hundred-meter butterfly — first place, Julie Swenson, Marlin Beach. Sec—"

But the rest got drowned out by the roar of the Marlin Beach crowd. Mom and Dad were hugging each other and wobbling the board we were standing on by jumping up and down.

Julie and Irene — still in the water — had arms draped over each other's shoulders and were talking intently. You'd think they'd be bitter enemies, but the fact is when they're not in the middle of a race against each other, they're pretty good friends. Swimmers are really each other's family. Basically because they're the only people who can stand to *talk* for hours about something as boring as swimming after *doing* it for hours.

I stood there watching everyone else hugging each other, and suddenly felt completely alone in the world. Where was *my* family? I snuck off, like I was going to get a can of soda or something, walked off through the Surfcrest gates, and headed across town to Joey's.

Chapter 6

Joey lives in a trailer with just his father.
His mother died in a car accident before I
met him. His dad works construction jobs
and takes a lot of overtime, so he's gone
most weekends, and doesn't get home until
late at night. This means that Joey winds
up living pretty much on his own.

He buys his own clothes, and does his
laundry down at the "mat," as he calls it.
He knows how to cook several dinners.
Hamburgers and frozen vegetables is one.
Baked chicken with baked potato is another.
He's a pretty good cook.

I go back and forth. Sometimes I think
Joey's life is extremely cool — getting to
come and go as he pleases and watch as
much TV as he wants. Other times I get
depressed thinking of him in that old
trailer, with only his old cat, Boston Bean,
for company.

The trailer is lopsided. I stood on the

little step hanging beneath the door and had to hold onto the doorknob to keep my balance.

"Jo-eeeeeey!" I called through the screen door.

"Hi," he said. "Step back down and open the door so I can let you in."

Inside it was like an oven — hot and dark and airless. Boston Bean woke up on the couch back, stretched like he was coming out of a hundred-year nap, then closed his eyes and went into another one.

"Might want to open a window," I said, wrapping my hands around my throat to show I was suffocating.

"I've got the air-conditioner on," he said. This is one of Joey's big delusions — that the old air-conditioner in the living room part of the trailer does anything besides make a huge amount of noise. He actually thinks it makes the air cooler. It doesn't. It's always either a hundred degrees inside the trailer, or a hundred and ten degrees, depending on whether it's winter or summer.

"So, what happened to you last night?" he said. "The dancing icicles got all out of formation because their tenth little drip was missing."

"No!" I said, half believing him.

"No," he admitted. "Everything went fine. I called when I got home."

"Yeah. I heard the phone. I was just too depressed to talk to anyone. Even you. My parents completely forgot the pageant. They were in some major crisis over Julie's turn."

"Her what?"

"Never mind," I said. I just wanted to change the subject. Thinking about last night was just getting me all steamed again.

"I didn't even bother telling *my* dad," Joey said. "By the time he gets home at night, he's too tired to make it through a TV show. I couldn't ask him to sit through a pageant. So, did you go to Julie's meet this morning?"

"Yeah," I said, as I flopped down on the prickly plaid sofa. "She won."

"Great," he said, taking off his glasses and wiping them with the end of his T-shirt. I was surprised he didn't make one of his usual sarcastic comments. Joey thinks my sister's swimming is this colossal waste of her youth; that when she's twenty she's going to look up and everyone else will have had all this fun and all she'll have is a bunch of medals and waterlogged fingertips.

"We're supposed to go see Mr. Bozo today," I told him.

"Oh. Okay."

Something was odd about Joey today.

Well, something is odd about Joey *every* day. But this was something different. He was being so unusually meek. I couldn't figure it out.

"Joey? Is something bothering you? I mean something besides knowing you're going to be spending one of the possibly great summers of your life working at a miniature golf course?"

"Uh . . . well," he started, then stopped. "I mean no. Not really."

I gave up.

"Come on," I said. "Let's go. I'm getting chilled sitting in front of the awesomeness of this air-conditioner. It's probably bad for my health."

He gave me his "very funny" look and opened the door.

I guess, as miniature golf courses go, Mr. Bozo's is a fairly nice one. It's new, anyway. Dad's friend, Steve Edmunds, built it only a year or so before we moved here.

"Nice color scheme," Joey said to me in a low voice, as we entered through the orange and yellow candy-striped archway.

Steve Edmunds was in his tiny office in the back. He looked like a bear in his cave. He is a huge guy with an almost completely bald head. It's hard for me to describe him any better because I'd never seen him out of his Mr. Bozo outfit and makeup — clown suit and huge floppy feet and white grease-paint on his face. His eyebrows are furry orange semicircles. They can't possibly be his real ones.

He seemed truly happy to see us.

"Things really start hopping here in the summer with all the kids out of school. I was glad when your dad said you two could help me out."

He told us what he'd pay, which wasn't all that great, but it was better than baby-sitting money, especially without the cleaning bills from all the stuff the McMahan kids spilled on me. Then he told us our duties.

"You'll have to keep the carpets vacuumed and pull balls out of the water traps and rent out putters and generally help people along so there aren't any traffic jams."

"It doesn't sound too hard," Joey said.

"It's not," Steve Edmunds assured him. "You've just got to be heads-up. Pay attention. Help me keep things running smoothly."

Then he rummaged around in some boxes behind his desk, and handed us our costumes. Mine was a polka-dotty happy clown suit with a red ball nose. Joey's was a hobo clown outfit.

"When do you want us to start, Mr. Edmunds?" I said.

"Call me Mr. B."

"Uh. Okay. When do you want us to start, Mr. B.?"

"What about now?"

"Oh, boy," Joey said to me, as we headed toward the washrooms to change. "It's like I'm cursed. I hate costumes and last night I had to bounce all over the stage dressed as an 'uggie.' I barely get back to civilization and I find out I'm going to have to spend the whole summer dressed up like Bob the Bum."

"If you got a job at the McDonald's, you'd have to wear a stupid polyester uniform and say 'May I help someone?' about two thousand times a day. I don't see that this is any worse."

He thought about it, and looked glumly down at the tattered coat and baggy pants and toeless shoes he was holding in his arms. He looked up at me kind of pitifully and said, "I don't really have to chew on this rubber cigar stub, do I?"

Actually, although I could never tell him, Joey looked kind of cute as a hobo. And the work turned out to be not too boring. In the late afternoon, people really started coming into Mr. Bozo's. By early evening, the place was full, with people waiting to tee off.

Renting the putters and fishing balls out of the water traps were the easy parts of the job. Keeping people moving along was the hard part. You would not believe the stupid trouble people can get themselves into on a miniature golf course. Three kids hit their balls right past the wide open clown's mouth where they were supposed to go, and straight through this tiny hole, into the roof of the windmill. It would've been amazing if you could've trained one kid to do this with a year's worth of practice. Three kids doing it by chance in the same afternoon should've gone into the *Guinness Book of World Records*.

The windmill sits in the middle of this little pool of water, and the only way I could get inside it was to roll up the legs of my clown suit and trudge through the knee-deep water, then open the little side door and squeeze through. I wasn't even really supposed to do this. Technically, if someone loses his golf ball, the game's over for him. But these were all little kids and they were only on the third hole out of eighteen, and when they found out they were finished so soon, they started crying and wailing and making really miserable scenes that made me hope the McMahan kids never showed up at Mr. Bozo's.

The third time I was inside the windmill was just before closing. I had just waded across the little moat and was looking around in the dark of the windmill for the lost ball when all of a sudden Joey came through the little opening from the outside. The interior space of the windmill is about like a short phone booth and so there we were, stooped over, crammed in there.

I looked at him questioningly. He looked back at me with this scrunched up and basically anguished expression I'd never seen on him before.

"Meg," he said.

"Joey," I said, dramatically, like someone in a soap. I was trying to get him to lighten up, but he just kept on looking tortured. And then he pounced. All of a sudden I was on the receiving end of this huge kiss.

"Joey!" I said.

"I love you, Meg," he said, looking deep into my eyes in this way that made me incredibly nervous.

"Oh, no!" I said. It was my first reaction. I realized just after I'd said it how awful it must've sounded. Joey jumped back — away from me — and hit the wall, then straightened up and hit his head on the rafters. Then he looked at me with this awful, hurt expression that I knew had nothing to do with hitting his head.

"Oh, Joey," I said. "I'm sorry."

But he was already out of the windmill and jogging through the course, and through the windmill window I could see him leap the fence and head toward town.

Chapter 7

"Your friend sure made a quick getaway," Mr. B. said to me when we were in the pro shop after closing, lining the putters up in their slots against the wall.

"Uh," I said brilliantly, groping for an excuse for Joey. "Well, I think he had to rush home. He takes care of his little brothers and sisters and he said one of them was sick."

"Oh. I see. How many brothers and sisters does he have?"

I didn't hesitate even a second.

"Seven." I made a mental note to tell Joey about his "family," so he wouldn't get tripped up later by Mr. B.

"Do you think he'll be coming back tomorrow?"

"Oh, I think so," I said. "I know *I* am. I really like working here." This wasn't a lie.

I really had enjoyed the day, and I could already see my money stacking up in a high pile. By the end of the summer, I figured I'd have enough to fly up to Minneapolis for a visit with all my old friends. Plus enough for some cool new clothes to wear up there. This was my big plan.

After I said good-night to Mr. B., I walked over to the Jungle Rapids to wait while my dad finished up his accounts for the night and gave me a lift home.

I climbed up to the top of the fake mountain and sat on some AstroTurf under a plastic palm tree and looked out. At night like this, with all the lights off, you could almost feel like you were on top of a real mountain. And I was high up enough that I could see over the highway, past the wild seagrass on the other side, all the way to the roaring blackness that was the ocean.

What I was thinking about, of course, was Joey. I thought I should probably try to track him down. I figured he'd either be at home, or playing video games at the Fun Zone. He's a video junkie.

The problem was, I didn't know what I could say if I *did* find him. He had pounced on me, hoping I'd be thrilled, and instead I'd reacted as if he were the maniac in *Friday the 13th*. I knew he must be feeling terrible, but I couldn't think of anything I could say that would make him feel any better.

If I tried to smooth things over, he'd know I was just trying not to hurt his feelings. And I didn't want to lie and say I loved him madly, because I didn't. I had exactly in mind who I was going to fall in love with, and it wasn't Joey. The guy I was going to fall in love with was tall and thin and had a great sense of humor and was a terrific dancer and an artist. A sculptor. He had dark red hair and green eyes. He had a wonderful name like Justin or Gregory. I hadn't met this guy yet, but I knew I would, and when I did, it would be love at first sight.

I could never fall in love at first sight with Joey because I'd already seen him too much. I'd done his laundry with him. I knew he wore this stupid plaid underwear. I'd brought over orange juice and Kleenex the time he had the flu, and sat all day with him while he blew his nose. It would just be impossible to fall in love at first sight with someone you'd already seen when they had the flu.

And besides, Joey was my best friend. I already loved him in a completely other way. Can a person just make that jump from friendship to romance? Absolutely not, I thought, until I remembered that

Joey had apparently made that jump quite easily. Without me even noticing.

I tried to look back over the past few weeks — for signs that Joey had been falling in love with me. But as hard as I thought, I couldn't think of any. Just last week, he had refused — as usual — to give me any of his popcorn at the movies. He was incredibly selfish about his popcorn. He said that whenever he *did* let me have some, I'd take all the top pieces, the ones with the butter on them, and leave the dry little hard pieces in the bottom for him. (I'll admit there might be a kernel — if you'll pardon the pun — of truth to this.) How can someone be falling in love with you and not want to give you any of their popcorn?

And then I remembered something. For months now, Joey had been crazy from afar about Lydia Freeman. She barely knew he existed, but he could tell you what Lydia wore to school on any given day. He was planning on working up to asking her out to the senior prom, which was three years away. But it occurred to me that Joey had not mentioned Lydia for a few weeks now. At least not to me.

And then I also remembered one night when we'd been out getting pizza, and I'd worn a jean jacket, and as we were leaving Ciao Bambino (all the restaurants around here have incredibly stupid names), he tried to help me on with the jacket, as if we were coming out of some swanky nightclub and he was in a tuxedo and helping me on with my velvet wrap. I'd just shrugged him off at the time and wondered if he was getting mature and mannerly or something. But now, it looked like there *had* been little pieces of the puzzle, and I just hadn't seen them. Or maybe hadn't *wanted* to see them.

"Sugar?"

It was my dad — the only person in the world who called me Sugar. It was sort of his nickname for me ever since I was little. I both thought it was hideously corny, and kind of liked it. I nearly jumped out of my skin when he said it now, though. I'd been so deep inside my thoughts that I hadn't heard him climbing up the mountain behind me.

"Dad!" I put my hand on my heart to slow the beating.

"Oh. Sorry. Didn't mean to scare you. I just didn't know where you'd gone off to."

"I was just contemplating the view from the top of my personal alp."

"See," he said. "There *are* some things down here that you like. This phony mountain. Your friend Jimmy."

"Joey."

"Right. And now you've got this great job for the summer."

"Oh, yeah. Cancel college for me, will you? I think I've found my true calling." I wasn't always this sarcastic with my father. But when he tries to get all upbeat about what a great decision bringing us all down here turned out to be, I get pretty mad.

He didn't see that I was mad, though — just that I was mouthing off, which makes *him* mad. He turned and started down the mountain without me.

"If you want a ride home, I'm leaving now," was all he said to me. In the car, he put the radio on loud and sang along to the oldies station. I guess my dad and I have what you'd call a "communication problem." It looked like I was beginning to have a few communication problems.

Chapter 8

The next day was Sunday. I didn't have to be at Mr. Bozo's until two, and so technically I could have slept in all morning. But I guess my body clock was still set for school and so there I was at seven-thirty — wide awake. No one else in the house would be up for hours. Especially not Julie. Once after a meet, she had slept fifteen hours. We were all pretty amazed.

If I was going to do something, it would have to be by myself. I had a brief flash-thought of calling Joey, and then I remembered — with a kind of thud inside myself — yesterday's scene in the wind-mill.

I threw on some shorts and a T-shirt and went downstairs. While my cheeseburger was getting waved, I filled a little backpack. I put in the Sunday comic section, a can of root beer, a towel, my sketchbook, and when the oven went "ping" I took out the cheeseburger and tossed it in the pack, too. I'd have myself a little picnic for one.

I got my bike out of the garage and rode down Marlin Avenue, which is the main drag in town. The only signs of life were the few early risers having breakfast at Kathy's Kitchen, the diner on the corner of Marlin and Jasmine.

Outside of town, I took the turnoff for the beach road, and pedaled past the older, more worn-down little houses that were here before Marlin Beach was really even a town, when it was just a gas station and the Flamingo Motel and Alligator World.

It was barely eight-thirty when I got to the cove, but Adelaide was already there, feeding her gulls. She really loves these birds and even has names for a lot of them. Mickey and Minnie and Donner and Blitzen. Romeo and Juliet. I told you she's pretty odd.

"Come on down!" she was shouting to them, like Bob Barker on *The Price Is Right*. And they were. I suppose because they like Adelaide (or some gull equivalent of "like"), but probably more because of the big hunks of old white bread she was scattering around the beach. They would swoop down on the bread in this formation that looked like a flapping white sheet and then soar back up again.

I sat down and pulled my cheeseburger

and root beer out of my pack and watched the action for a while. When the bread was all gone and the gulls had disappeared into the blue hole of the sky, Adelaide sat down next to me and sighed. After a few minutes she looked over at me, quite startled, as though she'd only just realized I was there.

"Lost your little buddy boy?" she said. "First time I've seen you here by yourself."

I could have just said that Joey was sleeping in this morning, or just that I felt like coming by myself for a change, but instead I poured out the whole story. Maybe I subconsciously figured that Adelaide was a safe person to tell — that she wouldn't tell anyone else my embarrassing dilemma, and that she'd give it her serious consideration.

"The thing is," I told her, "I could never in a million years fall in love with Joey, but I want him to stay my best friend. Still, now that he's made this big, heartfelt confession, I don't see how we can just be friends. He'll just be wanting to be my boyfriend, and I'll just get nervous knowing that. The whole situation is just about as awkward and stupid as you can get."

"It's a lot like gulls," Adelaide said, and my heart sank. She was just going to give me some crackpot, nature-related theory that wouldn't do me any good at all. But then I gave her a kind of "get-real" look and she thought a little more and tried again. She's like that — up in the clouds — but you can get her down to the ground pretty easily.

"Then again, maybe it's not at all like gulls. I think what you have to do is go talk this over with him."

"Why?"

"Because that's what friends do."

"Oh, Adelaide, I couldn't. I'd be too embarrassed." I was sort of hoping I wouldn't have to *see* Joey again until we were both about forty and we'd been married to other people for about twenty years and we bumped into each other at Sears while we were buying gas grills.

"The more time you let go by, the harder it'll be. And the more hurt his feelings will be. He must be feeling pretty weird out there all alone."

"Okay," I said, and reluctantly got up to go. Adelaide flipped up the little sunglass flaps on her glasses and looked at me real intently, then said, "Sometimes, you know, it's kind of fun to do the hard thing. Instead of taking the easy way out."

I nodded, although I didn't see the remotest possibility of fun ahead in this talk with Joey.

Still, I dutifully went looking for him. He wasn't at the trailer. I knocked on the door until my knuckles were red, but the only signs of life from within were the wheezing of the old air-conditioner, and Boston Bean meowing out the window at me a couple of times.

I checked my watch. Nine-fifteen. The Fun Zone opened at nine, and so that was probably where Joey was. For someone living in a sunny, outdoorsy, healthy place like Marlin Beach, Joey is about as outdoorsy as a goldfish. Nearly as great a lover of darkness as Dracula. On a super-nice morning like this one, with the breezes rustling through the palm fronds and the air salty from the surf spray, Joey was almost sure to be the only kid in town hunched over a video game in the cavelike depths of the Fun Zone.

Sure enough. I found him way in the back. It was a testament to our friendship that I went in there to find him. I hate video parlors. If someone wanted to drive me mad, they'd just have to lock me inside the Fun Zone for an hour. All the lights and noise completely fry my circuits.

Joey was playing Elevator Action, his favorite. He's really good at this game. This seems a pretty feeble accomplishment to me, but he says he likes getting his initials on the screen. This seems even more pathetic. I mean, it's like the tiniest bit of fame imaginable.

He didn't notice me come in. I put a

hand on his shoulder. No response. So I knock-knocked on his head. This did the trick. He looked up at me, a little stunned, then said, "Oh. Hi." The little video guys in the video elevators kept going up and down looking for each other, while Joey started losing about a thousand points a second, I guess. He didn't seem to care. He just kept staring at me. This was a little alarming. I mean, if my presence could distract him from Elevator Action, this was more serious than I thought.

"What's up?" he said, trying to sound terribly casual, but coming off more twitchy and tense than usual. Joey is absoultely terrible at faking cool. He went to lean against the game and missed it with his elbow and so instead fell against it with a crash. He straightened himself out, but I knew he must be feeling so stupid inside that he probably wanted to die.

"Can you come outside with me?" I said. "This place makes me crazy."

"I guess," he said, shoving his hands into the pockets of his cutoffs. To give you an idea of how uncool Joey is, he'd cut these jeans himself, but way too short, so the inside pockets hung down a couple of inches below the denim. But Joey thought these shorts were perfectly fine.

"I'll take you to McDonald's for breakfast," I said to him, as he was unchaining his bike from the lamppost outside the Fun Zone. "I thought maybe we could talk."

He nodded.

"I *do* have something I wanted to say," he told me, swinging a leg over the crossbar and taking off ahead of me. I followed him the three blocks or so to the McDonald's.

He wanted an Egg McMuffin and so I ordered him one, and just got myself a Coke. I brought the tray over to the booth he found for us by the front window. At first he just ate, like there was nothing to say. Then he said, "I'm sorry."

"What for?" I asked.

"I took you too much by surprise. I didn't give you any time to think about this. *I'd* been thinking about us for weeks and so I was real ready. But I didn't take you into account. It wasn't fair. So I apologize."

"Well, my response wasn't exactly the greatest, either."

"It was because you felt ambushed and overwhelmed."

"Partly it was because I felt ambushed," I said, trying to phrase the next part very carefully. "But partly it was because I don't feel the same way you do."

"But how can you be so sure?" he said. "You haven't had time to give the idea a chance."

"Joey," I said. "Falling in love isn't something you give long, careful consideration to, like which college to go to. It's just something you do impulsively."

"Well, that'd be okay with me," he said. "If you just fell for me in this big impulsive rush or something."

"But I'm not *going* to fall in love with you. And don't ask me how I can be so sure."

"How can you be so sure?"

"I just can. I know exactly the kind of guy I'm going to fall for. And I know it's not you. Which doesn't mean I don't love you. I do. You are my best friend, my kindred spirit. I couldn't have made it through this year down here without you. And I'm truly flattered that you are interested in me. But for me, the fact is that you are firmly planted in my 'friend' compartment. It's just too late to lift you out and put you into my 'boyfriend' compartment. Which I couldn't do anyway, because you aren't tall and thin with red hair. You aren't artistic. You see, I have this all planned. It's not your fault. I already had the plan way before I met you."

He put down his McMuffin and looked at me in amazement. I thought maybe it was because he found what I was saying so profound and persuasive, but then he said, "That is the stupidest thing I've ever heard you say."

"You don't have to be insulting," I said indignantly.

"Okay, okay. I'm sorry. But really. How can you plan out your life in advance? What if this artistic, redheaded guy never comes along?"

"I guess I'd have to modify my plan. Settle for an artistic blond."

He shook his head in disbelief. "Look. I realize that yesterday was too much too soon. All I'm asking now is that you give this a chance to happen. Just keep your mind open to the remote possibility of falling in love with a short, stocky, brown-haired, unartistic person."

I sighed. "Anything's possible, I guess."

"That's all I want you to say now. That it's possible, on this planet, in this dimension, in our lifetime, for you to fall in love with me."

"Okay. It's possible."

"Good." He finished off his breakfast in satisfied silence.

"But you've got to promise me — " I started to say.

"No more pouncing," he said.

"Not only that. You've got to promise you'll try to act normal around me. Like you always have. Like a friend. And then if I do fall in love with you anywhere along the way, I'll be sure to let you know."

He was nodding all the time I was laying

out these ground rules, and so I really thought he had a pretty good grip on what I was saying. But then when I was all finished, he looked at me with this real sincere expression and said, "Can I write poems to you?"

I left him at the McDonald's with everything in this loose-ends kind of state, and biked home. I thought maybe — since Julie usually got a day off after one of her meets — my family might be up for doing something together. A cookout or going shopping at the Egret Mall.

"Hey!" I shouted through the house, but no one answered. Odd. Sundays everyone was usually around. Double odd was the kitchen, which was in the middle of breakfast: toast popped up out of the toaster, eggs all fried in the pan, a pitcher of orange juice on the table next to an open Sunday paper. It looked like a scene in one of those horror movies where the interplanetary visitors hover over the house of the average family and beam the whole family up out of their life in the middle of whatever was happening.

I looked around for a note but couldn't find any. I slid open the glass door of the family room and went out into the backyard. Nobody was there either, but there *was* another sign of weirdness. The garden

hose was lying next to my mother's poinsettia beds, with the water just running.
The beds were pretty well flooded. I was
starting to get this creepy feeling all
though me. Like I was suddenly starring in
my own episode of *The Twilight Zone*.

Just then the phone started ringing inside. I dashed for it and picked it up before
it had rung twice.

"Yes?!" I shouted into it.

"Meg. It's Mom. We're all over at the
hospital. Julie's had an accident."

"What kind of accident?!"

"Apparently she was out riding on a
motorcycle. With some boy we don't know.
No one knows quite what happened. He's
in worse shape. A concussion, they think.
Julie just broke her leg. Of course, this
puts her out of commission for the whole
summer. I called Ian, but he's so angry he
won't even come down here. What was she
thinking of? Doesn't she realize that mega-
athletes with her potential have no business
jeopardizing themselves for a little fun?"

"I'll be right there," was all I said, but
inside I was screaming on my sister's be-
half, *What about mega-athletes who also
happen to be regular teenage girls? Don't
they get to have a little fun, ever?*

Chapter 9

I was in such a rush that I almost got into a couple of accidents myself on the way over to the hospital. First I went through a stop sign I didn't see, making this guy on another bike screech to a stop about two feet away from me. And then I came around a corner and nearly ran over two old guys pulling those wire shopping carts across the street. By the time I finally got to the hospital, I was completely out of breath and a little shook up.

I dashed into the main entrance, ran up to the desk marked "Visitors," and said, "I'm Julie Swenson's sister." Like everyone at the hospital was expecting me. Like I was some big celebrity — Johnny Carson or the President. I figured that, in this particular situation, acting like a big cheese would get me in to see my sister, and fast.

As it turned out, I was dead wrong.

The receptionist just looked at me like I barely existed, like I was a glob of protoplasm. Then she flipped through these little patient cards she had in front of her. Then she looked back up and through me and told me she couldn't give me a pass.

"Swenson already has two visitors. That's the limit. You'll have to wait until one of them comes down."

I nodded real seriously. There was no point in trying to argue with this woman, I could just tell. But as I nodded, I managed to get a glimpse of another patient's card. Gertrude Prince. She had *her* two orange visitors' passes stuck in the little plastic sleeve with her card.

"I ... uh ... I guess I'll get a cup of coffee while I wait. Is there a cafeteria in the hospital?" I asked politely.

"Down the hall and to the right," the receptionist told me. I headed off in that direction, but went instead to the gift shop — which had everything I needed. Sunglasses, a head scarf, and a small bouquet of flowers.

By the time I got back to the reception desk, I had my disguise perfected and my accent all ready. I have a small repertoire of terrific accents — French, Spanish, even Swedish. For this situation, I thought a nice southern accent would do the trick. You'd be amazed how few people in Florida have them, even though we're about as far south as you can get.

"Ah, excuse me, ma'am," I drawled softly. "But I wuhnduh if ah might pay a l'il visit to mah sweet l'il ole aunt?"

The receptionist — who had never really looked at me the first time — just looked through me again and said, "What's your aunt's name?"

"Gertrude Prince. Mah de-ah Aunt Trudy."

With my orange pass in hand, I got into the elevator and stuffed my disguise into my backpack. I found my sister's room right away, but almost thought no one was there, it was so quiet as I walked in.

But my mom and dad were both there, sitting in these high-backed vinyl visitors' chairs, not saying anything. Julie was propped up in a hospital bed, looking pretty bruised up. There was a bandage on her right cheek and her poor leg was in a cast, suspended in midair by cords with weights and pulleys. She was staring out the window.

"Great view," I teased her. She was looking out over the hospital parking lot.

All three of them looked up at me.

"Meg, honey," my mom said.

"Come here, Meggers," Julie said, and gave me a big hug when I got there. "Boy, you must've flown here. Oh, and with flowers! Wow."

"Did you turn off the hose in the back-yard?" my dad asked me. Mr. Practicality. Plus, I could tell, it was a subtle signal to not open up the subject of the accident — clearly the subject everyone was avoiding.

I told him I'd gotten the hose.

"And I locked up before I left," I added. Then I went over and sat on the other bed in the room, which was empty. I asked my sister if her leg hurt.

"A little," she said, but in this tight voice that made me know it was more than just a little.

"Can they give you a pill?" I'd had my appendix out in this big emergency a couple of years earlier and so I knew that if you really hurt in the hospital, you could usually get them to give you a pill, and that it helped.

"Why didn't you tell us you were in pain?" my father asked Julie.

"Maybe we should call Ian and clear it with him first. You know how he likes to supervise Julie's medication, even if it's only an aspirin," my mother said.

I felt like screaming at her. This whole business of "Julie the Swimmer" was an area where my parents — otherwise rational people — became like robots under the command of The Coach. And so I just ignored my mom's concern and went out into the hall, where I asked the nurse on duty if they could bring Julie a pain pill.

She checked Julie's chart and then said, "Sure."

"Why don't you guys go get a cup of coffee or something?" I told my parents when I got back. "I'll stay with Julie."

They looked at each other and agreed.

"I suppose we might as well," my father said. "We don't all have to be here at once."

No sooner had they left than the nurse came in with the pain pill, which was perfect timing because Julie could just pop it in her mouth without a half-hour discussion about whether or not his Royal Highness Ian Braithwaite would approve.

It took her a little while, but I could tell from the way her face un-scrunched that my sister was feeling better.

"They're really mad at me," she said. "I mean, about two seconds after they found out I wasn't dead, they moved right into being furious."

"They care," I said. "You know they do. They're just a little overabsorbed in this swimming thing."

"Sometimes I think they're more involved than I am."

"Julie!" I said. It was the first time I'd

ever heard her say anything slightly negative about swimming.

"Meg. What do you think I am — a machine that moves through the water? I'm a person. I'm a girl. And lately, especially, I'm beginning to feel much more like a *girl* than a swimmer."

It took me a second to get what she was really saying. Sometimes I am thicker than a Bombay Elm. The deeper meaning of this statement — I could now see — had to do with Brad Hunter.

"How is he?" I asked.

"I don't know for sure," she said. "I asked Mom and Dad, but at first they wouldn't even talk about him. Then later they told me he had a slight concussion — but can a concussion be slight? Maybe he's in some kind of serious condition and I don't even know about it. I even thought of trying to get ahold of some crutches and sneaking down there myself. . . ."

"Yeah, it's pretty easy, sneaking around on crutches. And really good for multiple fractures, too," I told her sarcastically. "Get real."

"But if I can't go myself, how am I ever going to find out how he's doing?"

Now, thicker than a Bombay Elm I may be, but I can still tell when my sister is finagling me into doing something for her.

"You want me to sneak down and find

out for you," I said, hazarding a wild guess.

"Oh, could you?!" she said, like it was all my idea, and a terrific one at that.

"Yeah, sure. But what'll we tell Mom and Dad?"

"I'll say I wanted a couple of magazines and you went down to the gift shop to get them for me. Then when you come back, you can tell me how he's doing. In code. Like, if he's basically okay, you go over to the window and say, 'My what a beautiful day!' If he's in bad shape, look out the window and say, 'Looks like rain.' Okay?"

"Okay," I said dubiously. This plan seemed pretty half-baked to me, with a lot of possibilities for something going wrong, but Julie was anxious for me to get out of the room before my parents came back up from the cafeteria. She was also getting a little goofy on account of the painkillers, so I knew I wasn't going to be able to get her to work out a more foolproof plan right now anyway, and so I just scooted out of the room.

I found the nice nurse. For a second I thought that maybe being a nurse would be a good career idea for me, and then I remembered that I couldn't stand to see anyone get a shot (especially me), or look at even a drop of blood without feeling faint, and so I scratched that idea.

"Uh, could you tell me what room my

sister's friend is in? The guy who was in the accident with her? Brad Hunter?"

She scanned her charts and found him.

"Four-oh-eight. End of the hall." She pointed the way for me.

I don't know what I was expecting, but he looked much worse. Bruises all over, his head all bandaged up. He was hooked up to an IV, and looked like he was out cold. His mother was sitting next to him, looking truly tragic. Somehow you don't think of tough guys like Brad Hunter having mothers who chuck them under their chins or rumple their hair or bake their favorite cookies or whatever. But there she was. She had red hair and kind of a lot of makeup, which by now — from all her crying, I guess — had run down her cheeks. I didn't want to come crashing into someone's private space, so I started to back out of the room. But she'd already looked up and seen me.

"Hi," I said, always the brilliant conversationalist.

"Hi. Are you a friend of Brad's?"

"Uh, sort of. I'm Julie's sister."

"Oh, yes. I hear she's all right."

"Well, I don't think she's going to be down at the disco tonight, but basically she's okay."

"I'm glad. Please tell your parents I'm

sorry about this. I wanted to get down there myself, but I haven't wanted to leave him."

I nodded to show I understood. I didn't want to ask the obvious question — how was Brad? Although it seemed rude and insensitive not to, it also seemed kind of insensitive to ask, especially if he was dying or something. But then, while I was debating this in my mind, she just went ahead and told me.

"Bratty's going to be all right, too, they say."

Bratty!? I thought. I could hardly wrap my mind around Brad Hunter having a teddy-bearish childhood nickname.

"He had a concussion," his mom was going on, "but he regained consciousness almost right away. He's been sleeping for a while. They want him to rest. I wonder . . . ?"

"What?"

"Could you sit here and keep an eye on him while I go down the hall and call my mother? I want to let her know he's all right and I can't make a long-distance call from the room phone."

"Oh. Sure."

"If anything happens, just push the call button for one of the nurses."

"Oh, right," I said, sitting down right

next to Brad, and taking the call button in my hand so I could be right on the spot if anything went wrong.

Asleep, Brad looked very sweet, almost like a little boy. I thought, maybe this softness is a hidden side of his personality that he shows to Julie. That would explain better why she liked him so much.

I tried to imagine Joey having a hidden side to his personality, some mysterious depths that would totally surprise me. I tried to imagine this but couldn't. I just knew him too well. Like the back of my hand. Like the route I took to school every day.

After about ten minutes, Brad started moaning a little, softly, and rolling around. I was about to push the button. I thought maybe this was a turn for the worse. But then he opened his eyes and looked right at me. I could tell he didn't have any idea who I was.

"It's Meg," I said to help out. "Julie's sister."

"Julie," he said in this far-off, dreamy way. "Julie. Love Julie."

And then he closed his eyes and went to sleep again. I checked to make sure he was only asleep by putting my ear close to his mouth — to see if he was still breathing. Which he was.

When his mother came back, I sat around with her for a little while, to give her some company.

"This kid is never getting on a motorcycle again, I'll tell you. I didn't raise him all by myself all these years just to have him die in some stupid, senseless way. He's got such a terrific future ahead of him — college, then law school."

Law school?! This was even weirder information about him than the "Bratty" part.

When I got back up to Julie's room, she looked at me searchingly, but it seemed too weird to leap into the code right away.

"Where are the magazines?" my mother said, and I felt like a total dolt.

"Oh, I ran out of here so fast, I forgot to take my money. I'll go back down in a minute."

I looked over and Julie was motioning toward the window with her head. Not exactly subtle. Then I remembered she was on that stupid pain pill, and was probably going to keep acting like Goofy until I gave her the information she was dying for.

And so I went over to the window and blurted out, "It certainly is a beautiful day." The words weren't even all out of my mouth before I realized a sudden storm had come up, and it was pouring rain in front of me.

This caused Julie to burst out laughing, and keep on with it like she was never going to stop. My parents just sat there looking at the two of us. I figured what the heck, I'd already messed up so badly that nothing I said now mattered very much, so I told Goofy, "And the beautiful day says he loves you."

Chapter 10

One night a couple of weeks later, I came home beat after a long day at Mr. Bozo's. Mr. B. said it was his biggest day ever; nearly three hundred people had putted their way through the course. It seemed more like three *thousand* to me — most of them under seven years old. But I didn't say anything. I didn't want to burst Mr. B.'s balloon.

He was going on about how miniature golf was going to be the leisure activity of the future. Joey and I just nodded and acted real enthusiastic and then — surprise! — he gave us each a five-dollar bonus for the day, which was great.

I said good-night to both of them and rode my bike right over to the cash machine outside the bank, and deposited my five dollars. Where money is concerned, I am a complete tightwad. Not even my parents know how much I have saved from baby-sitting the McMahan kids, and now from this job. Julie suspects, and is always leaning on me for "emergency" loans. She tends to have a lot of "emergencies." Really dying for a cheeseburger at the Burger Boy. Desperately needing some white shorts she saw in the window of Crickets. I always give her the money, but I charge her a pretty steep interest rate — compounded daily. I'd told her she had to pay me back by the end of the summer, so I could pay for my trip up to Minneapolis.

She was there when I came in — sitting in front of the TV with her leg propped up on the ottoman in front of the old rattan chair. This wasn't too surprising. She'd been practically glued to that chair since she'd come home from the hospital. Her cast was so heavy that getting around was a huge deal. Getting to the bathroom and back took her about half an hour.

She was alone a lot of the time. Her old boyfriend Tom Bauser was staying away with a vengeance. I guess after the accident everyone told him what Julie hadn't been able to — that she was involved with someone else now.

That someone else was still in the hospital, but due out any day now. Julie talked on the phone with him every day. Those low, muttering kinds of conversation where you can't really hear a word, but you still get the general idea. She had to talk to him on the sly, when our parents weren't around. Even the name Brad was poison around our house. Once my mom came in unexpectedly and I had to take the receiver and pretend to be talking to the dry cleaners about some pants they'd lost. (A total lie.)

The first few days after she got out of the hospital, friends of Julie's from Surfcrest stopped by with flowers and funny cards. A couple of the girls brought a Trivial Pursuit game and played it with her for an afternoon. But after this initial rush, these kids more or less stopped coming. Maybe they are such athletic types that being cooped up in a living room with a person in a huge cast just got them too restless. Maybe they couldn't relate to Julie in the same way, now that she was immobilized. Like it made her a different person. Dopes. The only visitor who kept on coming was Irene Hofstadter, Julie's archrival, who, as I may have mentioned, was about the nicest person in the world once she was out of the water. But Irene lived all the way up in Boca Verde and so couldn't really get down here all that often.

My mom and dad and I all noticed that Julie seemed to be getting a little lonely.

"She's begun to talk about characters on *The Young and the Restless* like they're real people," my mother said. "That can't be a good sign."

And so the three of us rallied around. My mom started teaching Julie how to cross-stitch, and got her going on a set of pillowcases with little pine trees on the borders. At the rate Julie's going, they should be done sometime around the year 2000.

Then my dad taught her how to play gin rummy. They played every morning before he had to go to the Rapids — for imaginary, but very high, stakes. Julie turned out to be quite a gin player. My dad owes her over $50,000 now.

Of course, my folks have always paid Julie a lot of attention, but this was different. This had nothing to do with swimming. For the first time in years, they were just hanging out with her, as a person — and when I was around, hanging out with me, too. It was nice, sort of like this trip we all took out West three summers ago. Being together hours and hours a day in the car, we got pretty chummy, and the same thing was happening this summer.

Nobody was home except Julie that night, though. I flopped onto the sofa and asked, "What's happening?"

"Mom's over at the Rapids helping Dad clean the chutes."

"Yeah. I saw them on my way home. I just bent over my handlebars and rode real low. I don't think they saw me. The last thing I want to do after a killer day at Mr. B.'s is scrub down the Rapids. Does this make me an awful person?"

"Yes," Julie said. "And an ungrateful wretch of a daughter. And as soon as they get home, I'm going to tell them that was you sneaking by."

She was only teasing. Julie would never tell on me, even if I robbed a bank. We'd made a secret pledge when we were little kids, and have never broken it in all the years since.

"Oh," she added. "Joey called."

This didn't seem like a major news flash. I'd just seen him not twenty minutes ago, and so I just sort of filed the information away under "not terrifically important."

"You know," I told her, pulling off my running shoes and then my socks, and tossing them in the middle of the living room floor. This was sure to get me yelled at when my parents got home, but right then I was too tired to care. "It would've been much more appropriate if *I'd* gotten the broken leg. Then you could've swum your way merrily through the summer while I loafed through it like the true couch potato I am. Plus, I wouldn't have had to involve myself in the wonderful world of miniature golf."

She shook her head in this pitiful way and said, "Don't wish this on yourself. Even a three-toed sloth like you would go crazy after a few days."

She seemed so dejected. I started trying to think of something that might cheer her up a little.

"You going to call Joey?" she said, nagging at me a little.

"Sure," I said. "Tomorrow."

"He said it was important. He sounded pretty serious. He didn't do that duck impersonation like he usually does."

"Oh, okay," I said, groaning as I pulled myself off the sofa and went into the kitchen to call him from the phone in there. I just have to punch two buttons to get his number. He's number nineteen on the automatic dialer on our phone. When he saw this, he was insulted. You'd think he'd have been flattered to rate a spot on the automatic dialer at all, but he just griped that he was after "Drugstore" and "Weather."

It rang twice and then his father picked it up.

"Hunh?" Mr. Moss said, completely out of it. I'd woken him up. I hate when this happens. I almost hung up, which is my usual, chicken-hearted way to deal with tricky phone moments, but if Joey really needed to talk to me, I figured I had to get through this.

"Uh, hi, Mr. Moss. Is Joey there?" Then I added, "I'm returning his call," to kind of shift the blame onto Joey.

"Right," he said groggily, then dropped the phone. Not just the receiver, the whole phone. The noise just about broke my eardrum.

"Hi," Joey said when he finally got on the line.

"What's the big emergency?" I asked.

"No emergency," he said in this new, kind of smooth voice. "I'm just calling about tomorrow night."

"What about tomorrow night?"

"Wellll . . . it is your night off at the course, isn't it?" To call Mr. B.'s "the course" was really ridiculous. The whole tone of this conversation was very weird.

"Uh, yeah, I guess it is," I said. "So what?"

"So I'd like to know if you'd go out with me."

"What do you mean?" I asked. "You want to watch TV over at your place like usual?"

"No, Margaret," he said, calling me by my real name, which as I may have indicated, I hate like poison. "I mean, would you like to go on a *date* with me. Like girls usually do with guys."

"Oh," I said, then couldn't think of anything else to say.

"Well?"

"Well, I guess. But what's the point?"

"Does there have to be a point?" he said. "Can't you just go along with me on this?"

"Oh, all right," I said, probably not in the friendliest tone of voice. "If you promise not to call me Margaret ever again. If you do — even if we're in the middle of this date — I'll have to punch your lights out."

I came back into the living room.

"What'd Joey want?" Julie asked, pulling her attention away from *Cagney and Lacey*.

"We're going on a date," I said. "And if you tease me about it, I'll have to kill you, even though you're a helpless invalid."

She just nodded. Another great thing about Julie is that she knows when to lay off. Now, she just nodded her head toward the TV.

"The drug dealer Cagney's just busted turns out to be Lacey's nephew," she said, and motioned for me to sit down and watch with her.

The next day went along in a perfectly normal way — I worked on a new drawing and played checkers with Julie for a while, then washed her hair, which is nearly impossible for her to do by herself with the cast on — until about six o'clock. That's when I started getting all nervous in this weird, fluttery way.

At first I couldn't believe it. But there it was, like a bunch of butterflies whooshing around underneath my rib cage. Even though I was just going out with Joey, who I went out with about five times a week if you counted bike rides and hanging out at the cove and waiting with him while he did his wash at the laundromat. And then I realized exactly what was happening. I was being influenced by the power of suggestion around the word "date."

Even though this was probably going to be the dumbest date in history, its being a date at all was getting me incredibly nerved up. Of course, it was also my *first* date. Ever. And so I suppose that was a factor in my jitters. But still. Really. I mean, give me a break — was I turning into a mush-brained, goony girl? When I prided myself so much on being a hard-headed, clear-eyed person?

"Get a grip," I said to myself in the mirror.

"You are talking to yourself," my sister said. She was thumping by the open door to the bathroom as I spoke, and overheard me. "I thought you'd want to know," she added.

"Julie. Why am I even one bit rattled about this stupid date?"

She shrugged, or made as much of a shrugging motion with her shoulders as a person can when they're on crutches.

"Not sure. Maybe you like Joey more than you think you do."

I thought about this possibility for a moment, then shook my head.

"Nope. I don't. Actually, at this particular moment, I like him quite a bit less than I usually do — for making me go out on this joke date."

"Well, your part of it will for sure be a joke if you go like that."

"Like what?" I said indignantly.

"In those old cutoffs and with your hair not even washed. What if Joey shows up in a jacket and tie? What if he brings flowers?"

"Believe me," I told her. "I know Joey Moss like the back of my hand, and he's not going to be dressed up or be bringing any bouquet."

And so, of course, he showed up in a jacket and tie, holding a box with this incredibly sweet gardenia corsage in it.

"Uh," I said about as brilliantly as someone who'd just gone into shock.

Julie called helpfully from her chair. "Meg's running late. She had to help me wash my hair. Come on in and talk with me while she finishes getting ready."

Finishes?! I thought. I hadn't even started.

I rushed upstairs and took a fast shower and blew my hair dry on the blowtorch setting. Then I took the stairs to the attic two at a time and pulled about eight possible outfits out of the closet, tried them all on, and finally settled on my best sundress, which is navy and contrasts nicely with my blonde hair (if I do say so myself). Then I ran down to Julie's room and swooshed myself with her Jontue.

I stood for a minute in front of the full-length mirror she has on her closet door and thought that I didn't look too bad. That is, I'm no raving beauty, but this was probably as good as I got. And I was kind of pleased to see that if I put in a bit of effort, I could pull off a pretty nice total effect.

Joey must've thought so, too. When I came down into the living room, he looked like somebody'd thrown a medicine ball at him. Bowled over is, I believe, the expression. Unfortunately, *both* my parents were also there by the time I made my grand entrance. Parents have this perverse sense of timing. Mine, for instance, who ignore me about ninety-nine percent of the time, picked this as the moment to focus on me.

"Well, look at this, will you!" my dad

said, just like I'd been hoping he wouldn't. "Meg's all dressed up! I never thought I'd see the day!"

"Johnny, *too*," my mother cooed in this "we-all-know-what's-going-on-here" voice that made me want to crawl under the sofa and die.

"Joey," I corrected her. Then I reached into my handy bag of lies. "Well, there's this banquet Mr. Edmunds is taking us to. The Miniature Golf Course Owners Association. They're presenting him with an award for most innovative windmill, and he insisted Joey and I come to help accept the award. We thought we'd better dress up."

I could see Joey looking at me with questions popping behind his eyes like flashbulbs, but luckily he knew enough to keep quiet.

"Oh," I said, getting into my lie now, "I see Mr. B. sent a corsage along for me. How nice of him."

"Uh. . . ." Joey started to say as I grabbed his arm and propelled him out of the house.

"Got to run!" I shouted back over my shoulder in this breezy, nonchalant voice, and kept propelling Joey like an outboard motor all the way to the sidewalk. When we got there, he turned on me.

"This is pretty insulting, you know. You

don't want your family to know we're going on a date."

"Joey, they'd just be awful — all 'oooo' and 'cooo' and 'isn't that cute?' Could you really stand going through that?"

"I don't know," he said, giving it some thought. "Maybe I wouldn't mind. And anyway, this is worse. This looks like you're ashamed of me — of going out with me, anyway."

I realized that what he was saying was true.

"I'm sorry," I said. "I guess I'm behaving so weirdly because this whole thing is a little weird. No offense."

"It *is* a little weird," he admitted. "But you promised you'd give it a chance."

I looked at him. He had such a hopeful expression on his face. Actually, in his sport jacket and pressed shirt and tie, his whole being radiated hope. I'd have had to be a real crumb to deflate his high spirits. And so I just smiled and linked my arm through his and said, "All right, Prince Charming. Cinderella's ready for her big night out!" I looked around, then added, "Now where are those mice and that pumpkin when you really need them?"

Chapter 11

"Where are we going?" I asked Joey as we stood on the curb in front of my house. "Do you have a plan?"

He nodded.

"First dinner, then a show."

"Sounds like a real date, all right," I agreed and headed off in the direction of the McDonald's. But Joey stopped me.

"Not tonight. This is a *major* date. I want to take you someplace that has table-cloths."

These tablecloths turned out to be red-checkered ones, draped over the tables at The Venetian Gardens Italian restaurant out on the beach road. On the tables were those candles in red glasses wrapped in plastic nets. On the wall was this big mural of a gondola coming down a canal. Basically, it was a place with a large amount of atmosphere.

Everyone around us was an adult, which

made it sort of cool being there. Of course, it would've been cooler still if the guy in the booth had been my dream guy with the red hair, instead of just Joey.

When the waitress had left us our menus, Joey opened his and said, "I recommend the spaghetti with meatballs."

"Why?" I thought this was a perfectly reasonable question, but it rattled him a bit.

"Well, I don't know. I just thought I'd say it because it seemed like the kind of thing the guy on the date ought to say at this point in the date." He sighed. "Actually, it's the only thing I've eaten here. Both my dad and I had the spaghetti when he brought me for my birthday."

"Joey," I said. "I wish you'd just relax a little. It's going to make me crazy if you keep up with this 'date' personality. It's too nervous-making — like being in a play with someone, only they have a script and you don't."

"But if I don't use my 'Suave Guy' manner, you'll just think it's the same old me."

"No," I lied. "Your tie and the restaurant have already gotten me in the spirit. I already think of you as a different person. So now you can just act like yourself."

"Oh, great," he said, exhaling as though he'd been holding his breath the whole time until now. "There's something I want to ask you."

"Shoot," I said.

"The other day, I put my new red T-shirt in the laundry. Now all my socks are pink. Is there anything I can do?"

You see what I mean. The mere idea of me getting romantically involved with Joey Moss is absurd. I *was* getting into the date a little, though. It was kind of a kick being dressed up for a change, and instead of having plain old spaghetti, Joey and I ordered a bunch of stuff we'd never heard of before. Calamari, which was good until we found out it was fried squid. Then we had Linguine Carbonara, which was like spaghetti, only the sauce was cheese and bacon. Really good.

The only stupid part was at dessert, when Joey reached across the table and took my hand. This meant I had to eat my spumoni left-handed, which was pretty awkward. I waited what seemed like a polite amount of time, then pretended that I had to cough and pulled my hand away to cover my mouth.

Then we went to see this new movie with Meryl Streep, whom I love and Joey hates, so I knew he was really trying to make the date nice for me. It was an incredibly hot night, still eighty, even though the sun was down. And so the first few minutes inside the theater were just this bliss-out of feeling all your molecules getting cooled down. After that, I snuggled down into my seat and really got into the movie.

Preoccupied as I was, I didn't notice any of Joey's big buildup. I didn't feel him drape his arm over my shoulders. I didn't see him take his gum out of his mouth and park it on an old popcorn bucket on the floor. By the time I saw what was going to happen, it was already in the middle of happening.

And so I got kissed a second time by Joey Moss. This time it was different from the kiss in the windmill, though. For one thing, he'd taken off his glasses so they didn't bump into my face. For another thing, this time he sort of took his time and didn't mash my lips, and so it was a softer, nicer experience. I just kind of let it happen to me and waited to see what I felt. Sort as if I were Dr. Jekyll in the laboratory, drinking from the frothing beaker, then waiting to see how I'd change.

Joey pulled his face away from mine, put his glasses back on, and peered intently at me through them. He has really thick lenses that magnify his eyeballs and make his expressions kind of exaggerated.

"So," he whispered. "What do you think?

"I'm not sure," I said honestly. "Much better than the other time. Pretty interesting, actually."

"Want to try it again?"

"Okay."

This time I kissed back, which made it better yet. I felt like we were really getting the hang of it.

Suddenly this woman's voice boomed out from right behind us.

"STOP THAT NECKING AND WATCH THE MOVIE!"

Both Joey and I slunk so far down in our seats we couldn't even see the movie screen. I looked over at him and we both burst into these uncontrollable giggles. I put a finger up to my lips to signal him to be quiet. Then I squirmed around in my seat so I could peek through the space between the seats and get a look at her.

There she was, looking at the screen, munching on a candy bar. She was a big woman with big hair — blonde and piled up on her head in these stiff curls. Like a country singer. The good news about her was that she wasn't anyone I knew. The bad news was that she looked like just the sort of no-nonsense person who wouldn't be the slightest bit embarrassed to shout at us again — for good measure.

"Let's get out of here. We can go sit up in the balcony," I whispered to Joey, who nodded and squeezed my hand to say okay.

I felt like a spy sneaking out of the row and up the aisle. Sort of daredevilish. In the lobby, we both decided we were hungry again and got some popcorn and a Coke to share. (This was another aspect of the "New Joey" — willingness to share his popcorn.)

Hardly anybody knows about the balcony and so we were the only ones up there. We just couldn't get rid of the giggles, and neither of us could pick up on the plot of the movie, having missed so much. And so we kept making these wild guesses as to what was going on. Which only got us laughing harder. I never could figure out the plot. Still, it was one of the best times I'd ever had at the show.

I told him that on the way back to my house.

"This isn't anything like what I thought a date would be like," I admitted to him, "but it was amazingly fun in its own weird way."

This seemed to make him happy, and so I didn't say the rest of what I was thinking — that it had been a lot like an experiment, kind of a test run for what I still imagined a *real* date with the *right* guy would be like.

I came in hoping my mom would be hanging around the kitchen. I sort of felt like having one of those TV sitcom kind of mother-daughter conversations. You know. Where the mother asks, "How did your date go, honey?" And the daughter just blushes and doesn't really say anything, but it gets the two of them into this little late-night chatty mood. They have some cocoa and the mother starts remembering her *own* dating days.

Something along those lines is what I was looking for as I came though the door. I should say that I've never had a conversation remotely like this with my mother. I guess my hopes were up a little because of how friendly things had been getting around the house lately. Some of the times I'd hung around her and Julie while they were working on their cross-stitch projects, we had actually gotten into some pretty funny conversations. Mom had started to ask us questions about ourselves — what we thought of this or that. I thought she was starting to get to know us a little, which felt really nice.

She wasn't in the kitchen when I came in, though. She and my dad were in bed watching David Letterman. I could hear the TV from the front hallway. She did come out onto the landing, though, and called down to me, "That you, Meg?"

"Yeah," I said, then stood there for a moment, thinking maybe she'd come down.

"Don't forget to turn the dead bolt, will you?"

"Oh," I said. "Okay."

As I stood there in the flat, stuffy dark of the hallway — so still I couldn't even hear myself breathe, I started crying. Not sobs or sniffles. It didn't even feel like anything I was doing — more like the tears were happening *to* me, sliding hot and wet down my face and I was just powerless to stop them.

Why — just once — couldn't my mother surprise me by acting like I was an interesting person, someone she might want to know more about? And if she couldn't do that, I'd even settle for her liking me — not for anything particularly great about me — but just because I'm her kid.

I mean, when you see interviews with mothers of twelve-year-old genius chess whizzes, or mothers of those rock stars who come onstage with live snakes wrapped around their necks — they always say "he was such a sweet boy, had a little paper route and a kitten named Puffy." These mothers don't understand their kids at all, but they love them anyway. And yet here I was, an easy-to-understand, incredibly interesting person (once you got to know me), but I couldn't get any more attention from my mother than her telling me to be sure to lock the front door.

It just wasn't fair.

Chapter 12

About this kissing I did with Joey. I just
want to say that it did *not* — like it always
does in movies — make me suddenly go
crazy for him. I didn't feel any differently
about him at all, really.

I did, however, feel quite a bit different
about kissing. I liked it a whole lot more
than I'd imagined I would. Plus I was feeling a little smug. Like I was a woman of
experience now. I didn't say anything
about any of this to him, or to anyone.
Not even to Julie. For some reason, I
needed to keep it to myself for a while.

I started planning my treat for Julie.
There weren't too many places I could take
her. Basically, taking my sister anywhere
these days was like moving an odd piece of
furniture, or a small building. A gazebo.
Finally, though, I came up with the bril-

liant idea of a picnic. I got up early on Sunday to make it.

As you may have noticed, I lean pretty heavily on the old microwave in my cooking. I wasn't really sure how to put together a real picnic lunch, so I poked around in my mother's cookbooks and found one with a section titled "Dining Alfresco." From the photos, it looked like this meant picnics.

I skipped over all the hard recipes — anything that called for "de-boning" chickens, "reducing" sauces, or "julienning" anything. I made a list of what I'd need, rode my bike over to the Winn-Dixie, and brought my supplies back in my basket. With the help of the blender, I made a really nice lunch of deviled eggs, vichyssoise (really cold cream-of-potato soup), iced tea, and little sandwich triangles filled with cream cheese and cucumbers. I was pretty proud of myself.

All this high-power cuisine *had* made a pretty big mess of the kitchen, I must admit. And (bad luck!) my mother walked, still half asleep and heading for the Mr. Coffee, right into the middle of it. This did not put her into the best of moods.

"What's this?!" she said, scanning the counters full of eggshells, potato peelings, onion and cucumber skins. "Did the garbage disposal back up again?"

"Uh, I'm just getting to the cleanup part," I said, rushing around a bit, pushing stuff off into the wastebasket. "I'm taking Julie on a picnic."

I pointed at the stuff I was about to put into a big paper grocery bag. My mother looked at the jug of soup, then unwrapped a sandwich, then clicked her tongue at the deviled eggs.

"None of this is on her diet," she said.

"But neither is Julie," I said. "I mean, she's not swimming this summer, right? Can't she be on the Depressed-Person-in-a-Big-Cast Diet for a while? Can't she have a few treats?"

"*Meg*," my mother said, in that tone of voice that is never followed by anything good, "Julie's body is a fine-tuned piece of machinery. Like a Porsche. Even though she's off her feet for a while, she still has to keep in shape as much as possible. And you shouldn't be sabotaging her."

"Sabotaging?!" I said. "I just want to cheer her up a little. Come on. Please. It can't hurt, just this once."

She looked over the picnic stuff again, thought for a minute, then said, "Okay. But leave the eggs behind. Way too much cholesterol." Then she looked around the kitchen again. "Here's a plan. I go back upstairs for fifteen minutes or so. Then I come back down and you have all this cleaned up."

"Right," I said.

She ran her hand over the top of my hair on her way out. "It's a nice idea, Meg," she said, softening up a little. "Julie'll like it."

I took Julie to the closest possible picnic spot — Douglas Park, just a couple of blocks away. It's not one of the seven wonders of the natural world. It's not Yosemite or the Everglades or anything like that. Actually, it's more of a playlot than a full-scale park but still, it seemed to make Julie really happy to be there, just to be outside after these couple of weeks of being cooped up.

"You must really miss the outdoors and moving around — and swimming," I said to her when we'd made it over there and found a bench and got Julie off her crutches and sitting down.

"Well, my *body* does, that's for sure. Even if I go just a couple of days without swimming, it starts saying, 'What's going on here? Let's get in the water!' But in another way, it's nice to be off the hook for a while."

"How do you mean?" I really didn't know what she was talking about.

"Well, I am kind of under a bit of pressure at home. From Mom and Dad."

"At least they notice you," I said, probably sounding a little more whiny than I'd like.

"Notice me?!" Julie shrieked. "They *peer* at me. Scrutinize me. Observe. Advise. Frankly, their being so mad at me, and Ian giving me the freeze-out treatment, has been a relief in a way."

I was beginning to see our family situation in a new light. I'd always thought of my parents' attention as a spotlight shining on Julie, with me standing off in the shadows. Now I could see that the person standing in the spotlight also had to take the heat.

"But I thought *you* were into swimming, too," I said, setting the jug of iced tea between us and rummaging through the bag for the plastic cups I'd brought along.

She tilted her head back until she leaned it on the top edge of the park bench, her face to the sun, her eyes closed.

"I don't know," she said in this vague, eerie way. "I don't know anything anymore." Then she sat back up and faced me. "I've been swimming since I was two-and-a-half. I don't know what a life without it would be like. But sometimes lately, I pull my head out of the water and look around and see that most girls my age are having an awfully good time."

"Yeah, but most of them aren't going to be in the Olympics."

"There *is* that," she admitted, picking up her cup of tea and taking a sip. "Mmmm. Good. Odd, though. What's in here?"

"Well, I didn't have any lemon, so I squeezed a peach into it."

She laughed, but then admitted it was pretty good. "And original."

"You're not thinking of quitting? Swimming, I mean?"

"It would be pretty dumb, don't you think? Especially now, when I'm so close. Not to mention that Mom and Dad would kill me."

We were quiet for a little while, and then I asked her something I'd never asked her before. "Do you ever wonder who your real parents are?"

I guess I was expecting her to say no, because I was really surprised when she said, "Of course."

For some reason, this made me sad. I'd always figured that Julie was happier in our family than I was. So why was she wondering about this *other* family? Plus it made me feel a little rejected. She must've read my mind because right away she started in on me.

"Yeah," she said in this dreamy, far-off voice, staring into the distance. "I guess it's more that I like imagining how it would be having a really cool sister. Someone who was cheerful and friendly to everyone. Someone who liked to go swimming with me. In my mind, I call her 'Jennifer.' Our names would sort of go together — Julie and Jennifer."

I lunged over the picnic bag and started tickling her. Julie goes insane when you tickle her, begs for mercy, which is what she started doing now.

"The cast! Watch out for my cast! Don't tickle the infirm!"

"I'll stop," I said, noticing that we were getting a few stares from a few of the other people around us. "But only if you promise to be serious."

"I'll be serious," she countered, "but only if you'll give me my lunch. I can't stand the suspense."

I pulled everything out of the bag and set it all up — pouring the vichyssoise into little mugs, setting the sandwich triangles and egg halves on these great old paper lace doilies I found in the bottom of my mother's drawer of party stuff. It really did look nice, all arranged like that on the green wood slats of the park bench. Kind of English, if you know what I mean.

"Oh," Julie said, looking at her picnic, "it's so sweet. I take it all back about

Jennifer. You're the best sister I could ever get — even if our names don't match."

"Thanks," I said. "But tell me the part about wondering what your real parents are like."

"I don't exactly have a father in mind, but my mother is this really easygoing type with no big plans for me. She's pretty young and we hang out together a lot. We go shopping and to the beach, and then just grab dinner at some fast-food place."

"Jennifer comes along, too, I suppose."

"No. She's in college up at Gainesville. She comes down on weekends in her Corvette, and gives me makeup tips."

"How does she afford a Corvette?" I asked. It seemed like a reasonable question.

"It's just a *fantasy*," Julie said, then added in this kind of embarrassed voice, "Actually, Jennifer and I have *matching* Corvettes."

"Sounds like a pretty advanced fantasy," I said.

"It's just a little escape valve," she said, then added, "I mean, I hardly ever think of actually going to look for my real parents."

I was stunned.

"But you *do* think of it sometimes?" I asked, and could hear my voice squeak, which it does sometimes if I'm nervous.

"Well, there are organizations that'll

help you," she said. "I saw a feature on the *Today* show."

I guess my eyes must have popped open, or my jaw had dropped, or something obvious. I probably looked like the explorer standing inside the ancient Egyptian tomb when the mummy starts rising out of its mummy box. She saw this look and got very serious with me.

"Meg. Everyone wants to know who they are, where they come from. For most people, it's easy. They just have to look around the house. Like *you*. You can look at Mom and Dad and say, 'Well, that's where I get my blonde hair, and how I can carry a tune, and the fact that I have long toes.' I don't know where any of me comes from. It's like I came from another planet."

"Like Superboy came from Krypton."

"Sort of. Only it's probably easier to have no past if you're a comic book superhero. If you're just a regular seventeen-year-old girl in Florida, it's a little weird. I'd kind of like to see them, talk to them, see how I'm like them."

"Your real parents," I said.

Julie nodded, then added, "And if they didn't know anything about swimming, maybe I could spend vacations with them." She stopped there and looked around for a way to change the subject. "Boy, this soup is great!" she said. "You made this?!"

I nodded.

"What a gourmet!"

This got me a little embarrassed, but I was also kind of pleased that my picnic was going over so big — it being my first *alfresco* meal and all.

"I want you to do me a favor," she said then, her voice taking on a new tone — like we were spies together planning a secret mission.

"Sure," I said.

"I got a get-well card for Brad. Can you take it over to his house for me? He came home yesterday."

"Oh, Julie, I don't know. I have to tell you I'm not too crazy about what he did to you." I motioned toward her leg. "I mean, some guy wants to take my sister out on a motorcycle, I say he ought to learn how to drive it first."

"*I* was driving," Julie said.

I gulped the sip of soup I'd just taken.

"I talked him into it. He didn't want to let me, but I told him I knew I could handle it."

"Boy," I said, then whistled this long, low whistle I'm good at.

"Boy what?" Julie said.

"Boy, you've really got this wild streak I never knew anything about."

"I'm really just discovering it myself,"

she said and grinned this sly grin. Another aspect of my sister I'd never seen before.

I took the card over to Brad's on my way to work that afternoon. As I turned the corner onto his street, I tried to pull my face into a serious, visiting-the-sick expression. But then, when I was still two doors away, I heard the loud chords of an electric guitar or two and a keyboard. The music — I'm using the term extremely loosely — definitely seemed to be coming from Brad's house.

I got all nervous. He probably had friends over. Wild guys he hung out with who would just look at me and my card — it was in this dippy pink envelope to make matters even worse — like I'd just landed from the planet Nerd. So I did what any brave and courageous messenger would do: propped the card against the door and prepared to ring the bell and run.

Before I could do this, though, the door opened and there was Brad's mother, all smiles and happy to see me.

"I saw you through the window," she said. "Is the doorbell broken?"

"Uh, no . . . I just dropped my card. I wonder if you could give it to Brad? I don't want to disturb him."

"Oh, I'm sure he and the boys'll be happy

to see you. They're all up there welcoming him home. Spider's here, and Bruno. Weasel, too."

They sounded like a great bunch.

"Uh, well, then I guess I'll just go on up," I said, heading toward the increasingly loud sounds of heavy metal rock being played badly. When I got to the door of Brad's room, they all turned and froze in mid-chord, and then just stood there silent and staring at me.

Brad was propped up in bed holding his guitar awkwardly. His arm was still in a cast, but his head wasn't bandaged anymore. Now there was just this little scar and a few bruises. He looked a lot better than the last time I'd seen him. I still couldn't quite get used to his regular looks — the earring and the stubble and the rat's tail in the back of his hair — or rather, I couldn't get used to them being the look of my sister's true love.

The other three guys in the room were weirder yet — especially the two-hundred-pound guy with the shaved head and leather jeans — and so I was glad when Brad smiled and said hi to me and then told the others, "Hey, guys, why don't we take five. This here's my girlfriend's sister. Give us a few minutes to chat."

When the imitation Beastie Boys had

trudged out, leaving me alone with Brad, I went over and handed him Julie's card.

"Thanks," he said, and motioned me toward a chair next to the bed while he ripped open the envelope. I could see as he pulled it out that it was a Smurf card. I felt myself going all red. I was totally embarrassed for my sister. Maybe spending all those years in the pool had taken their toll, and retarded her social development. This was a card for a six-year-old, not for the baddest guy in Marlin Beach.

But then, to my total surprise, he started smiling at the card — or maybe at what was written inside — and smiling in this completely goofy way. He looked up at me.

"Your sister's quite a girl," he said.

"Lousy driver, though, I hear."

"Nobody's supposed to know she was driving."

"I'm safe," I assured him, pantomiming locking my lips and throwing away the key. "The tomb of secrets."

"Tell me one," he teased.

"Nope," I said.

"Okay. You passed the test," he said. "Now tell me, how *is* the Terror of the Open Road?"

"You're not mad at her?"

He shook his head. "It was my fault, really. I knew she'd never driven a bike before. Luckily I had helmets with me, or we both would've been much worse off than we are." He pointed upward.

I nodded. For some reason, it was the first time it really hit me that Julie could've actually *died* on the motorcycle.

"You're really crazy about your big sister, aren't you?" he asked me.

"Yeah," I admitted.

"Me, too," he said. "I worry about her."

"Oh, I think she's going to be all right."

"No. I mean *after* she's all right, and your parents push her back in the drink and crack the whip and make her start swimming all those laps again."

"But Julie *wants* to keep swimming."

"I know. She wants to make it to the Olympics. But what kind of life is this anyway? I think she ought to have time for just hanging out, going to the beach, going out with me."

I could see that Brad really cared about Julie, and he did have a point about her life, but his concern also seemed a little self-centered. It sounded like what he wanted was a less swimming-oriented, more Brad-oriented Julie. And so, in a way, he was just one more pressure in her life.

I excused myself. "Late for work," I said, which was a lie, but only a small one. I really had just about enough time to get over to Mr. B.'s.

When I was at the door, Brad called out

to me. "Hey. I think my friend Bruno might be interested in you."

"Which one is he?"

"The big guy with the shaved head," Brad said.

"Gosh," I said, snapping my fingers in disappointment. "Too bad I already have a boyfriend."

Chapter 13

By the next morning, when I told Julie how much Brad had liked her Smurf card, she was already hatching a new idea. I'd just brought my breakfast — microwave fries and a glass of chocolate milk — into the living room, where Julie was reading an Agatha Christie mystery, lazily scratching under her cast with this unbent wire hanger.

"Meg?" she said, in this slow way that meant for sure she was about to ask me for something. Stuck in the easy chair most of the time, she would stack up her little wants, and then, when someone came through the room, she'd snag them into getting whatever — a Kleenex or apple or glass of iced tea — for her. You couldn't really get mad at her for this, but it was kind of a drag to never be able to make a clean run through the living room.

"Yeah?" I said now, sitting down on the sofa next to her.

"You must be getting pretty good at your drawing now, I mean, given all the time you spend on it."

I had no idea where this was leading.

"Well, sort of, I guess," I said, trying to sound vague. I'd never shown her any of my drawings, although I think she has gotten a look now and then when she's come up to my room.

"I was just thinking how cute it would be if I could come up with an original card for Brad. Something personal. You know, especially for him."

"And you want me to draw this card?"

"I'd pay you, of course," she rushed in. "Just add it to my account. Say two dollars? And you don't have to come up with the concept. I've already got that all figured out."

"Yeah?"

"Yeah. I want a picture of him on the front — you know, show his stubbly cheeks and his earring and his reflector shades. Can you do that?"

"I think so. It's not exactly my style, but. . . ."

"Great. And then above his picture, I want 'To Brad.' And then under the picture, 'A Great Lad.'"

It's a good thing Julie's trying to make

it as a swimmer, not as a poet. I didn't tease her, though. You could tell she thought this was a terrific rhyme. And Brad would probably love it. She could send him a peanut butter label and he'd go all goofy. The two of them were enough to make you decide against ever falling in love, just so you wouldn't have to go around looking that stupid.

"I'll do it tomorrow," I told her. "I'll do a nice job."

And I meant it. This was, after all, my first artistic commission. And so I wound up putting about three hours into the stupid card — doing the drawing of Brad in pen and ink, then filling it in with markers. I did the lettering by penciling in fine guidelines, drawing the letters along them in ink, then erasing the pencil marks. All in all, I thought it looked pretty sharp when I was done. But I didn't expect the reaction I got from Julie. If she hadn't been in a cast, I think she would've jumped up and given me a standing ovation.

"Wow!" she said. "This is just incredible. The picture looks *so* much like him! And it's all so artistically done. I mean, I don't know what I thought you were doing up there, but nothing like this! You've got to show me all your drawings. Come on. Go get them!"

"Well, uh — " I said, warming up to a little speech about how I wasn't really ready to "go public" yet. But she didn't even give me a chance.

"No 'wells.' Come on. I'm an invalid with a small wish. You can't refuse me."

"Okay," I said, and started up the stairs. Sometimes it struck me that my sister could get me to do pretty much anything she wanted. I mean, if she was a circus knife thrower, she'd probably be able to talk me into standing there holding up the balloons.

Anyway, when I brought my whole "Best" folder of drawings down, she raved even more about them than she had about the card. This was great because it let me know it was *my talent* and not Brad's face that sent her into these raves.

"This is a whole little world you've created. These unicorns and what are these. . . ?"

"Wood nymphs."

"And these little rabbity creatures. . . . Has your art teacher seen these?"

I shook my head.

"You've got to show her," Julie said.

"Okay," I said, sliding the drawings back into their big brown cardborad envelope. "When I get back to school in the fall."

"No, I meant now."

"Julie," I groaned. "It's summer vacation."

"So? You think teachers disappear in June — like birds at night? Let's call her right now. I'll bet she's listed. What's her name?"

Wild horses could not have dragged it out of me. But Julie managed to remember all on her own.

"Jenkins?!"

While she went through the phone book, I thought I might be the first person on record to actually die of embarrassment. Jenkins is my favorite teacher. She's young (twenty-five, I'd say) and basically just one of those people who are extremely cool without even trying. She's given me an A in her class, and always liked the projects I did there, but this was different. This wasn't just showing her my drawing ability — it was showing her this whole private world I'd created in my own imagination. What if she thought it was childish or stupid? And calling her at home, barging in on her with my "important" drawings. It just seemed too brash and nervy.

I knelt down on the cool terrazzo floor in front of Julie and put my hands in begging position, to try to get her to put the phone receiver down. But she was on a roll. She just kept punching the little numbers, and then — after what must have been quite a few rings — said in this bright and cheery voice, "Ms. Jenkins? Hi, it's Julie Swenson — do you recognize the last name? My sister has you for art . . . yes, that's right. . . ." At this point, Julie laughed, like she and Jenkins were old pals. Then she forged on with this Most Embarrassing Call in the World. "The reason I'm calling is my sister, Meg. Right. Meg Swenson. You probably just think of her as one of your students. You probably have no idea she's secretly one of the greatest artists in Marlin Beach."

This is where I died of embarrassment. You've seen in those supermarket newspapers where people die for a few seconds, then come back to life and tell all about it? Well, I can't tell you much about being gone, but when I came back, everything on earth was pretty much the same except for one terrible turn of events. Julie was now holding the receiver out to me for me to talk to Jenkins — and there was no way I could get out of it!

I took it reluctantly and said, in my cracking, nervous voice, "Hello?"

"Yes, Meg?"

"How are you doing?" I blathered on. "Are you busy? Am I getting you at a bad time?"

"No. I was just cleaning house. How are you enjoying your summer?"

"Oh, it's great. Except my sister got in an accident." She was concerned. I told her a little about the accident, and that everything was going to be okay. I was pretty chatty and informal. I almost thought I could get off the phone without mentioning my drawings, but when I looked over and saw I was being stared down by my sister, I just blurted it out really fast.

"Saywouldyoumindlookingatthesedrawingsofmine?"

"Pardon me?" Jenkins said.

I tried to go at a normal pace this time.

"Would you mind looking at these drawings of mine? You're probably too busy, resting and all. That's okay. Thanks anyway."

"No, I'd love to see them. Why don't you bring them over?"

"Oh, okay. When?"

"What about now? We can go over them while my freezer defrosts."

I'd never been to a teacher's house before. Actually, it has always been hard for me to imagine any of my teachers having another life outside of class. I mean, if I ever run into one of them — like at the 7-Eleven, or at the beach with their kids — I'm just astonished.

The address Jenkins gave me turned out to be a houseboat. There's this little community of them downtown in the harbor, but I didn't know anyone who lived on one. Well, I guess I did, but I didn't know it until then. Jenkins' houseboat was one of the smallest, but one of the cutest of the lot. It was painted blue with white trim and was called the *Matisse*. After the French painter, I guess. Jenkins is *very* artistic.

She was on the back deck when I got there, scrubbing away with a brush and bucket. She stood up to welcome me as I chained my bike to a utility pole on the dock. I was surprised to see she was wearing shorts and an old workshirt and a baseball cap. My dumb thing about teachers again. What did I expect — that she'd be scrubbing her boat in a dress, or in her painter's smock? Sometimes I am positively pea-brained.

"Hi!" she called out, then came over to give me a helping hand on board.

"Wow, living on a boat. Neat!" Then I realized how I must have sounded. Sometimes I think all my cynical detachment is just a hedge against the fact that I sound like an absolute nerd when I am really enthusiastic about something. Jenkins just seemed honestly pleased, though.

"Now, watch your head and come on down," she said.

I followed her down a steep set of little steps into the cabin of the boat.

"Iced coffee?" she offered when we reached the bottom of the steps.

"Great," I said. "Thanks." Then, while she went to the little kitchen at the end of the room to get it, I looked around. It was one long room, done up in an eccentric, artistic kind of way. The floors were wood, painted a shiny turquoise; the walls were dark red. The sofa was some kind of antique and covered in a printed fabric that looked like the feathers of a peacock. Paintings were hung on all the walls — all kinds of paintings. It was a pretty odd place, but I liked it.

"Neat," I told her when she came back with the iced coffee. "It's just about a polar opposite from my house. My parents bought all our living room furniture at the same time. It all goes together. *Nothing* here goes together . . . but in another way, it kind of does."

Either Jenkins liked this analysis, or she thought it was funny, because she laughed a little. Then she pointed toward my envelope.

"Those your drawings?"

"Mmmhmm."

"Why don't we sit down here and take a look at them?" she said, pointing to the floor where we were standing.

"Okay," I said, and got down and began pulling the drawings out, one by one, handing them to Jenkins, who looked at each one seriously and for a long time. Then she went through them all again. Through this whole time, she didn't say a thing, which began to get me a little nervous.

Then she was done. She looked over at me, reached across the drawings and rumpled my hair, and said, "Kiddo — they're brilliant."

"You like them?" I said stupidly.

"It's more than that. They're not just accomplished drawings. They show you've a particular — particularly wonderful — vision. Would you mind if I showed these to someone else?"

"Who?!" I said, as though the implication was that she wanted to show them to the police.

Jenkins laughed at my jumpiness, then reassured me.

"I have a friend on the local art scene. I think she might be interested in these. That is, if you'll trust me with them for a few days."

"Oh. Sure," I said, but I did look around at the houseboat with a scrutinizing eye, to see if it looked at all firetrappy.

Jenkins, who is pretty sharp, caught my glance and said, "Don't worry. I'll guard them with my life. If the place goes up in smoke, I'll grab my kittens and your drawings, and run."

I smiled with a mixture of feelings — relief and embarrassment and just being pleased.

We talked for quite a while. First about the drawings I'd brought, then about the plans I had for a new bunch about a world of friendly but shy creatures who only come out at night, when people are asleep and can't see them. Jenkins liked the idea.

"Your parents must be very proud of you," she said.

"Why?" I asked.

"Well, having such a talented daughter."

"Julie's the talented one in the family. I'm sort of the regular one."

"Believe me, Meg," Jenkins said, "no one who can conceptualize and draw like this is 'regular.' "

"Yeah, well, the drawings are just sort of this hobby I keep to myself."

"Not anymore," Jenkins said, smiling in this way that was nice, but a little mysterious, too.

I could have stayed around her houseboat for about a week. I was secretly hoping she'd ask me to stay and have dinner with her. But then she got a phone call from someone it looked like she really wanted to talk to (an incredibly cool, artistic guy, I'll bet), so I made a quick exit.

Coming down the dock, I almost ran smack into Jill Percival. She wasn't with Ron Mussman; just by herself. She was dressed in white shorts, white top, white socks, and very new (first wearing, I'd say) tennis shoes. She looked like she was about to step onto a yacht. Actually, she probably *was* about to step onto a yacht. At least she was heading in the direction of the part of the harbor where all the big cabin cruisers were tied up.

"Well, Meg," Jill said. I was kind of surprised she even remembered my name. "What're you up to?"

"Oh, nothing much."

"Your family have a boat docked here? I haven't seen you around before."

"No, I was just visiting . . . uh . . . a friend."

"Oh?" she said, just dripping with curiosity now. "Who? We know almost everyone who has a yacht here."

"Oh, no. Just someone who lives on one of the houseboats. Ms. Jenkins, actually."

"Jenkins?! Like, the art teacher Jenkins?!" she squealed, as if this was the most outrageous and unbelievable thing she'd ever heard. Jill is one of those girls who manages to squeeze the word "like" into just about every sentence.

"Well, yeah," I said, trying to make it seem like it was no big deal.

"You, like, hang out with teachers during summer vacation?! What's the deal? Are you some kind of teacher's pet or something?"

I figured this was a situation where the best defense is an outrageous offense, and so, "I'm an artist, Jill," I said in this theatrical voice. "I need to be part of an artistic community. I need the cross-pollination of ideas and style. Jenkins is part of that community, too. She is *simpatico*, as we artists say. Now, if you'll excuse me, I must get back to my easel! Art beckons!" And then I kind of swooshed off, as though I was wearing a cape, not just old gym shorts and a T-shirt. I could almost feel Jill's stare of amazement on my back as I went.

I felt pretty good about this little exchange. Jill would probably still make fun of me to everyone in her crowd, but I didn't care as much as I usually would. I was riding pretty high on Jenkins' praise of my drawings. I unlocked my bike, hopped on, and sailed off.

Chapter 14

The next week, my mom took Julie to the doctor and he pronounced her "mending nicely." He cut off her humongous old cast (which she saved for all the autographs on it) and replaced it with a new, soft one that only went from her ankle to her knee. The five minutes or so between casts was, Julie told me, "a total bliss-out of scratching."

"But, boy, does my leg ever look creepy," she added. "Real skinny and the skin's all scaly."

"It'll probably stay that way for the rest of your life," I said.

"Brad got his cast totally off yesterday," she said, ignoring me as she went into her love meltdown. "Don't you think that's, well, pretty symbolic or symbiotic or something?"

"You two ought to celebrate," I said. I was being sarcastic, but she was too in love to hear it.

"We talked about that, but neither of us can drive yet."

I stared at her in mild amazement. Something seems to happen to the teenage mind at the precise moment that it turns sixteen. Suddenly, the person who has all their life gotten around perfectly well by bicycle, or on the old, reliable feet, cannot get from point A to point B without a car.

I didn't point it out to her, though. I just decided to cook up a little non-car surprise for her and Brad. I stopped by Joey's on my way to work, to fetch him along, and talk to him about the plan. I had to practically break my fist pounding on the door. Finally he heard me over the air-conditioner.

"Door's open," he shouted.

He was on the sofa, watching TV with Boston Bean purring on his lap. Joey only watches the rerun channel. He likes the shows that were made before he was born. He says television's been going downhill ever since they cancelled *The Honeymooners*. This is one of the million peculiarities that make him such a charming friend, and which make him absolutely impossible as someone I could possibly fall in love with.

The guy I fall in love with will not watch TV at all. He'll read poetry and take me to foreign films. Afterward, we'll have long, deep discussions about them. He will be filled with sensitive thoughts on many subjects, which he'll share with me in phone calls that will run far into the night. The guy I fall in love with will never greet me as I come through the door into his living room by shouting, "Heyhey there, Ralphyboy!"

I didn't even acknowledge this as a recognizable form of greeting. I just went straight over to the minifridge in the trailer's minikitchen and got myself a can of root beer.

"My sister got sprung from maximum security," I told him. "Now she's just got this baby cast."

"Good," he said, his attention still glued to the TV. "Get her in the pool. Make her do a couple of miles on the kickboard." Joey the Cynic.

"Come on. Stop being weird," I said, sitting next to him on the sofa, picking up the remote and clicking off *Gilligan's Island*. I told him I wanted to put together a little treat for Julie and Brad. "Will you help?"

"Sure. I guess so." He sat up out of his usual slump. Boston Bean, sensing that he was losing his nap lap, hopped off and sauntered into the kitchen and began crunching away in his little rubber bowl of kitty biscuits. "What do you want me to do? Help make a little party? Bring the chips?"

"Something like that," I nodded. "Bring the chips. And Brad. Out to the cove tomorrow night."

"Brad Hunter?! Sleazy Rider?!"

"Come on. They haven't been able to see each other since the accident. We can play Cupid. It'll be fun. You just get Brad and the chips to the cove by eight. I'll bring the soda and Julie."

"I don't think it's a good idea to let other people in on our cove. They'll tell all their friends. Pretty soon the place'll be jammed with swimmers. They'll be playing water polo and driving all my fish away. And the dunes will be buzzing with dirt bikes. And the beach will be booming with boom boxes."

"Brad and Julie will promise not to tell anyone," I said.

"Wait a minute," Joey said, after thinking for a minute. "How are you going to get your sister to the cove — pulley her over the dunes on a skateboard?"

"How I get her there will be my little secret," I said smugly. "I am, as you know, extremely inventive."

He peered at me for a moment, probably waiting for me to spill my secret. But I didn't and finally he broke down.

"Oh, all right. I'll fetch Romeo and you

bring Julie-et. I'm always a sucker for a love story."

This time it was *Joey* who wasn't prepared for *me*. I slid his glasses down his nose and let them fall onto the sofa, then leaned in and kissed him.

It was great. Very soft and fluttery. Even with my limited experience, I think I may already be a fabulous kisser. A natural. Even with my braces and all.

There was something that bothered me a little, though. This time, right after the kiss — just for the tiniest slice of a second, but the feeling was definitely there — I did kind of feel romantic about Joey. I pulled back and looked at him and the thought that ran through my mind was: *Joey may have a croaky little voice and a goofy personality, but he has beautiful ears. They don't stick out at all. They just lie flat, looking so cute on the sides of his head.*

Then the reasonable part of my mind stepped back and told the goony part, *Get a grip, Meg.*

Chapter 15

Julie was really excited when I told her I'd cooked up a surprise to celebrate.

"A cast-off party," was all I'd say.

"Does this party by any chance include someone named *Brad*?" she said sweetly, trying to worm a little extra information out of me.

"If you ask any more questions, I'll make sure it includes someone named Schnellenbach." Mr. Schnellenbach is Julie's chemistry teacher. She thinks he's disgusting, plus he gives her Ds.

The only things I told her were to be ready at seven, to have a swimsuit on under her clothes, and if Mom and Dad wanted to know where we were going, it was over to Joey's to watch TV.

Luckily, they were both out when we left. Dad was still at work, and Mom had gone over to Sears to pick up some parts for one of our air-conditioners, which she was fixing. We left a note saying we were going to Joey's. I figured we'd just have to take the chance and hope she wouldn't call over there.

When we got outside, I made Julie wait while I went into the garage and came out with her barge.

"My little old red wagon!" she squealed. "I didn't even know we still had it."

"Your wheels for the night," I said, helping her off her crutches and down onto the blow-up raft I'd set inside the wagon. "I figure I can pull you about ten times faster than you can walk on those."

I tied the wagon's handle to the seat of my bike. It was a little rocky starting off, but then we were fine, aside from looking a little strange. We got quite a few stares as we cut through town. Julie is a much cooler social being than I am, and in the old days, she would've died sitting on a raft in a little red wagon being pulled by her sister on a bike. But the accident and the cast had gotten her used to being conspicuous, I guess. At any rate, she seemed to enjoy the ride.

When we got to the beach, it was sunset. They are pretty spectacular down here, and this was a particularly red one. We watched it happen, which it does in an instant. The huge sun is hanging there on the surface of the horizon and then — whoosh — it's gone.

I got out a plastic garbage bag and handed it to her.

"Put your clothes in this," I ordered her, like the commander on a secret mission. When she had peeled to her swimsuit, I did the same and put my shorts and tank top into the bag, too. Then I got her out of the wagon and put the raft into the water, then eased her into the raft. I wrapped her cast in some dry cleaners' bags I'd brought and taped around the edges. To keep the cast dry.

"Going for a ride," I said to her in a talking-to-baby voice.

I took the towrope on the raft and started pulling Julie out around the dune. I was hoping the water wouldn't get too deep, but after a while it did, and I had to use my extremely limited swimming skills.

"Meg!" she said from behind me. "You — swimming? I never thought I'd see the day."

"It was the only way I could think of to get you here."

"How does it feel?" she asked.

"A little scary," I admitted. I was trying to pull the raft and stay afloat myself. Plus, in the gray light of dusk, the water took on a vaguely creepy aura. I started worrying about what might be lurking beneath the surface. Jellyfish. Man-of-wars. Eels. The Loch Ness Monster.

"I know," she said. "Open water gives me the willies, too."

"You?" I said, turning around, getting slapped in the face by a stray wave. I spit out the water, sputtered a bit, and then regained my forward momentum.

"I've really only swum in pools," Julie said. "There, I know just how deep it is, and just how far to the end. And I can always see to the bottom. I'm kind of a goldfish, really. I think it is really brave of you to do this. Who knows what might be squiggling around there by your feet. . . ."

"Julie!"

"Oh. Sorry."

In a way, though, I was getting to like being in the water. There was something peaceful about just paddling along through the warm grayness. It made me feel dumb for having stayed out of the water for so long. What point was I proving, and how much fun was I cheating myself out of? I made up my mind to go snorkeling with Joey the next time we came out here.

When we rounded the dune, there was suddenly a bright glow surrounding us. Joey and Brad had apparently started a fire on the beach. It looked wild — orange and white against the gray-green of nightfall. We could see the two of them standing in the firelight.

"Oh!" Julie sighed behind me. "It's beautiful here. What is this place? How come I don't know about it?"

"Nobody does," I said. "Except me and Joey. You've got to promise not to tell anyone else."

"I promise," Julie said solemnly.

"Oh," she said then, looking up at the beach. "There he is." Brad Hunter is not exactly my dream of a guy, but clearly he *is* my sister's.

The guys waded out and pulled the raft up onto the beach for me. Brad lifted Julie onto her feet and held her by her arms while they looked at each other for this long, dreamy moment. It was kind of embarrassing to watch this, but kind of fascinating at the same time.

"Hi," Brad said. It was a "hi" that said about a hundred things more than "hi."

"Hi," Julie said back.

"Come on, you two," Joey said to me and Julie. "Over by the fire and dry off."

I'd brought a towel along in the plastic bag and got it out so Julie and I could get our clothes back on over our swimsuits. Then I fetched the six-pack of soda from the raft and put it on the blanket next to the fire.

Joey had outdone himself. Instead of just chips, he'd somehow managed to roll down that dune with a pizza they'd picked up at Ciao Bambino in town.

"Joey," I said, putting an arm around him.

"Catering by Moss, entertainment by Hunter," he said, pointing to Brad's tape player sitting on the blanket. Taking his cue, Brad punched the "play" button and suddenly the beach was awash in Lionel Ritchie. The mood was getting distinctly romantic. I thought, well, why not just go with it?

And it really was a lot of fun. We ate the pizza and let the fire die down while we listened to Brad's tapes. He and Julie talked a little about the accident. I could tell it still scared them, even just remembering it.

We all talked about Marlin Beach and how there was nothing to do there, for teenagers at least. Julie told everyone about Jenkins liking my drawings, and maybe something happening with them. "Something big," was how she put it. I could tell Joey was hurt that I hadn't told him anything about this. I would have, except I'm so superstitious. I never want to risk jinxing anything by talking about it before it's happened.

I squeezed Joey's hand in the dark, to try to signal him that I'd talk to him later. I think he was surprised that there was something in my life he didn't know about. Julie acted the same way a little later — about something else.

It was when the fire got down to just embers and it was so dark you could hardly see anything. She and Brad started kissing. It seemed pretty much a perfect opportunity for me and Joey to do a little kissing ourselves. I have to admit I was really getting into kissing Joey. I also have to admit it *was* changing the way I felt about him. I think it's because, when you start kissing somebody, they move into the position of "the person you kiss." Even if you didn't fall in love with them beforehand, the kissing definitely moves you along into love-type feelings about the other person. And it starts to put you in a love-type mood when that person is around. Especially if the setting is romantic.

That night, all these forces were so powerful that, in the middle of the third kiss, I began to get this vague, fuzzy feeling that I might actually be starting to fall in love with him.

I broke away fast, and looked first out

toward the ocean, which was rippling in this great silvery way it does in the moonlight. Then I looked over at my sister who — to my major embarrassment — was looking at me in wide-eyed astonishment. I probably should have told her somewhere along the way about me and Joey and the kissing. I guess I'd just been too shy.

None of us had a watch on, so we had to guess at the time. We didn't think it was too late, though, when we finally left — the guys by land, Julie and I by sea. Were we ever wrong! I guess, as they say, time sure does fly when you're having fun, because by the time we got back, it was eleven-thirty and I could see even through the front window that Mom and Dad were sitting there in a state of humongous furiousity.

Chapter 16

Julie and I tried to saunter into the house casually, like there was no problem.

"Let me do the lying," I whispered to her as I pulled the screen door open. Julie is the worst liar in America. Her eyes go all shifty and her voice starts wobbling. It's pitiful, really.

"Hi," she said to Mom and Dad. They'd been sitting down when we saw them through the front window, but now both of them were standing in the hallway waiting for us.

"Hi," I said, then stretched my arms up into this big yawn. "Boy, I'm really beat. Think I'll just go up and crash." I put my foot on the first step, heading toward my attic.

"Not so fast, young lady," my dad said. "First, maybe you two would like to tell us just where you've been all night?"

"Uhhhh," Julie said. I could see those eyeballs starting to shift like crazy. She was going to collapse under the pressure, I could just see it. I stepped in fast.

"At Joey's," I said matter-of-factly.

"We called there at nine, when Ian came by to see Julie," my mother said.

"Ian?!" Julie said, amazed. "What made him break his silent treatment, do you think?"

"He plays golf with Dr. Higgins, you know," Dad said. "He found out that you got your cast off and — "

" — he figures you're close to getting back in the water again," I piped up. "You were such a fool for getting in the accident he couldn't bring himself to speak to you. But now that you might get a couple of medals for the team, he can find it in his heart to forgive you." I knew this was pretty cynical, but where Ian Braithwaite was concerned, cynicism seemed the best approach.

My parents, on the other hand, thought Ian was practically perfect, and speaking against him practically a sin. They both turned on me at once.

"He came over," my mother said, glaring at me, "out of the goodness of his heart. To see how his little star was recuperating. But where was his little star? And don't

try to tell me 'at Joey's' because we called
there and his father said he hadn't seen
him — or you two — all night."

"It was too stuffy over there," I said.
"So the three of us took a walk."

"*Walking* was not exactly the descrip-
tion I got from Harriet over at the Winn-
Dixie," my dad said. "When I stopped
there for some milk on the way home, she
told me she'd seen my girls earlier — whiz-
zing past the store in 'an unusual contrap-
tion,' was how she put it."

"So then — just on a wild hunch — we
called Brad Hunter's house," my mom said.
"His mother said she didn't know where he
was, but wherever it was, he'd gone to meet
Julie."

I could see Julie starting to collapse.
There were tears forming at the corners
of her eyes. Sometimes she was such a
wimp. Pretty soon she'd be spilling all the
beans. About the wagon and rafting to the
cove. About the cove. She'd probably even
tell them where it was. For sure she'd tell
them Brad was there. If she really got into
the spirit of confessing, she might even tell
them about the camp fire and the kissing.
Her and Brad — *and me and Joey!*

I could see all this in a flash before my
eyes, and I knew she had to be stopped
before she could get started.

I leaped in with the single largest lie I've ever told.

"All right," I said in my most serious voice. "I know this is going to be hard to believe, but . . . we were taken by interplanetary beings for a visit on their UFO."

They grounded both of us for a week.

I hate being grounded worse than almost anything. As soon as I start thinking about it, I feel hideously trapped, like I'm truly in prison. And like all prisoners, I begin thinking about escape.

What I did was wait until everyone had gone to bed and the house was dark, its stillness broken only by the humming sound of the refrigerator downstairs in the kitchen. Then I got up and put on my sneakers and shorts and a sweatshirt and crept *verrrrry* slowly down the stairs. If I came to a place where the wood creaked under my foot, I just stood and waited and listened to make sure no one had been awakened by the noise. At this rate, it took me nearly twenty minutes to get down to the first floor. Once there, I could move faster, and slipped like a shot out the back door, got my bike out of the yard, and rode off toward Jungle Rapids.

A secret about me is that, even though I pretend that I think Jungle Rapids is the most boring way to spend time this side of watching paint dry, I really kind of like it. Especially when I'm all alone, late at night, in the dark. Double especially whenever I'm feeling weird or nervous or depressed about my life. Then I take a few night slides down the rapids. I have a key and just let myself in. I go into the control room and leave all the lights off, but turn on the water full blast. Then I get a mat and go up to the top, settle myself in the chute and let her rip — downdowndown through the black night.

Sometimes just doing this once is enough to cheer me up. But tonight I had a lot on my mind. I thought about how my feelings for Joey seemed to be changing in subtle ways I couldn't understand.

I thought about how much trouble I was in for all my lying. I was definitely going to have to cut back on it. Maybe quit entirely, although that was a little hard to imagine.

Then I thought about how, with Julie getting into competition again, things with my family were probably going to go back to the way they'd been before. Ian was already on the scene, with my parents practically kneeling and salaaming before him.

I could almost hear the gun going off to signal the restart of Julie's swimming career. Pretty soon everything around our house would revolve around her times and her technique and her diet and her workout strategy. And — just when I was beginning to feel like I had a place in the family — I'd be back where I was before: Off to the side, on dry land, unnoticed while everyone was facing the aqua excitement. I'd go back to being the fish out of water.

I sat on one of the little mats and made about twenty or thirty runs down the rapids — blind to the experience, just trying to get away from the hot pain inside me. But I couldn't. It was stuck there in my chest, and no number of slides down the chute could dislodge it.

In the end, I really just wound up wearing myself out instead of cheering myself up. I rode my bike the few blocks home at a snail's pace. Home. Ha-ha.

Chapter 17

The next day it was *really* hot out — ninety degrees before noon. But you almost didn't need an air-conditioner in my house. The atmosphere was frosty. My parents had cooled down from the night before — to ice. They gave me and Julie a freeze-out like I'd never seen before. Cold stares and chilly silences.

The rules of the grounding allowed me to go out only to work at Mr. Bozo's. Dad got my schedule from Steve Edmunds, so he knew exactly when I was supposed to leave, and when I was supposed to get home. Julie wasn't allowed to go anywhere at all. We both knew there was something essentially humorous about someone on crutches getting grounded, but it was hard to laugh at a joke when you were the punchline.

One part of the grounding I didn't know about was phone calls. Since I hardly ever make or get any, it was a few days before I figured out that mine were being cut off as part of the punishment. It was late one night when the phone rang. I was sitting in the kitchen reading this horror comic when I heard my dad pick up in the front hall.

"No, Shari," he said. "Meg's grounded for the week and can't accept calls. I'll give her the message over the weekend. She'll have to call you back then."

I ran out into the hall just as he was putting the receiver down.

"That was Shari and you wouldn't let me talk to her?!" Shari is my best friend back in Minneapolis. I was going to stay with her family when I went back north for my visit at the end of the summer. I loved getting calls from her, catching up on what everybody there was doing.

"It's cruel and unusual punishment not letting me talk to her."

"Well, you were *unusually* bad the other night," he told me. "Being a bad influence on your sister, taking her off to meet that hoodlum, then lying to us about the whole thing. And you haven't even apologized."

I thought for a while.

"I'm sorry for the lying," I said. "I can't be sorry for taking Julie out. She needed a treat, and I don't think Brad's such a hoodlum. He just *looks* and *acts* like a hoodlum."

I realized as soon as I'd said it that this probably wasn't the greatest defense. My dad, I guess, thought it was pretty funny. He started to smile, and then covered his mouth with his hand so I wouldn't see him letting his guard down.

"Hey, Dad," I said, as the thought suddenly occurred to me, "there haven't been any other calls for me — you know, that you haven't told me about?"

"I'll give you your messages on Saturday, when your week's grounding is up."

I could tell from the strict tone of his voice that there was no use begging or trying to cajole him into changing his mind. I could also sort of tell by the way he said it that there *were* other messages. Now I really did feel like a prisoner.

"Guess I'll go have some bread and water, then stare out the bars of my window for a while," I said, and didn't wait around to see my dad roll his eyes at my sarcasm.

I went through the kitchen and straight into plan B. The only important call I was waiting for was from Jenkins, about my drawings. All I had to do was trick my mother into telling me if she had called. It was pretty easy. I just sort of moseyed into the laundry room and asked if I could help out with anything. I actually like helping with the laundry, which is a satisfying job, as opposed to the dishes, which, around our house at least, seem to be dirty again about five seconds after you've put them all washed and dried up on the shelf.

My mom said why didn't I fold the clean sheets and towels on top of the dryer. I worked away in silence for a while, then said, nonchalant as could be, "Boy, I can't wait until Saturday. So I can return all my calls. Shari called tonight."

"She did?"

"Yeah. Maybe there's big news from the north woods. Oh, and I guess Jenkins called, Dad said."

"Right," my mom said. "She's your history teacher?"

"Art."

"Right."

Aha!

It was too late to sneak out and call Jenkins back that night. I had to wait until I got to Mr. Bozo's the next day. By the time I did, Mr. B. was closing down. What looked like a huge storm was coming up. I ran for the pay phone, which was surrounded by about a hundred squabbling kids waiting for their mothers to come pick them up before it started to rain.

"Hi, Ms. Jenkins," I shouted.

"Hi," she said. "What's all that racket?

Where are you calling from — a pay phone in a bowling alley?"

"Close," I said and explained.

"Your father said you'd been bad. Maybe I shouldn't tell you the good news. Maybe you don't deserve it."

"I probably don't," I told her. "But I sure could use it."

"My friend Clarice I was telling you about? She owns the Hubbell Gallery on Flamingo Drive. And she likes your drawings so much she wants to hang several of them in her Young Artists show next month."

"Oh," I said.

"You're not thrilled."

"Oh, I am. It's this stupid thing that I do, sound blank when I'm too excited. No, it's incredible. I thought you were showing them to another teacher, getting me in a special class or something. I didn't expect anything like this."

"She wants to get together with you — to set prices on the drawings. I told her you were grounded until Saturday. She said that waiting for one of her artists to get ungrounded was a first in her experience, but that it was no problem."

"She must think I'm pretty weird."

"Don't worry. The woman has dealt with artists all her life. They're all weird."

"Boy, I can't wait to tell my parents. But

I can't tell them I called you. It's against the rules of my grounding. I'll say you stopped by here — to play miniature golf. Is that okay?"

Jenkins laughed and said sure.

"Say, you'd better get on home. I'm looking out my window and it looks like *some* storm heading our way."

"Right. I'm going now. We're closing down here. But, hey, if you ever feel like playing a little miniature golf some other time, just stop by. I can always pass you in."

"Oh. Thanks, Meg. Thanks a lot." From the way she said it, I knew Jenkins wouldn't be caught dead playing miniature golf. I felt like an idiot for making the offer. Why didn't I just offer to give her a free ride down the Jungle Rapids while I was at it?

I told Joey about the show at the gallery. He gave me a big hug and was really happy for me, I could tell.

"I'll have to get you a beret," he said, then looked up at the sky, which was rapidly turning this eerie shade of yellowy-gray. "We'd better get out of here. You want me to ride home with you?" he asked.

"No. We'd both better get home while we can." Storms are one thing I'm truly afraid of.

* * *

By the time I got to my house, the rain had started and my parents were dashing around closing up the windows and pulling the shutters closed. Julie was upstairs reading in bed. I helped shut the windows and then I told Mom and Dad that Jenkins had stopped by Mr. Bozo's and given me the big news.

They didn't believe me. I mean they believed that Jenkins was playing miniature golf, which was actually the only *un*-believable part of the story. What they didn't believe was that I'd done drawings that were going to be hung in an actual big-time gallery on Flamingo Drive.

"What kind of drawings?" my father asked. "I didn't know you could draw."

"They're unicorns and other imaginary creatures," I said.

"Like the interplanetary visitors who gave you a lift the other night?" my mother said.

"This does have that Meg's-make-believe sound to it," my father said skeptically. "You'll pardon us if we don't fall for it this time."

I just stomped out of the room. I can do a pretty good stomp when I get mad enough. I guess something about how mad I got must have made my parents wonder if maybe I wasn't telling the truth.

At any rate, about an hour later, when I was up in bed, my dad came to the door of my room and knocked. I didn't answer.

"Meg?"

The lights were off and I just pretended I was asleep. This took a lot of stubbornness. I was terrified by the way the storm was thrashing around the windows and roof of my room, and would have loved someone to come and comfort me, reassure me about the storm, maybe take me down and make me some cocoa. Fat chance I'd ever get anything like that around here, though.

"Meg?" my dad said again, this time turning the knob and pushing the door open. I kept my eyes shut, but I could hear him come in and sit down in the creaky wicker armchair across from my bed.

"Honey. We talked to Julie. She told us those drawings of yours are really something. And then we called your teacher and she said it's really true about the gallery. So I guess we owe you an apology. It seems we have a real *artiste* in the house."

He stopped, I guess to see if I had anything to say to this, but I was silent as a stone. And underneath the silence, I was hot as a burning coal with all my anger.

"I guess there are a few things we don't know about you," he went on, in this innocent voice.

"A few?!" I shouted, sitting up like a shot.

"How come you never told us about any of this?" he asked, still trying to make it seem like it was all my fault.

"Why didn't you ever ask?" I challenged him.

"But you're always so secretive," he sputtered.

"Secretive?! Who's secretive? I've practically been shouting at you and Mom to get you to notice me. But around here, the noise of splashing and starting guns and the call of the Olympics just seems to drown out everything else. I've been trying to talk to you. YOU JUST WON'T HEAR ME!"

"B-b-but you've always been so self-sufficient," he said.

"Because I *had* to be," I countered. "Do you remember last winter when I got that earache?"

He thought for a moment, then said vaguely, "But then it got better by itself."

"No," I said in this cold, dead-calm voice. "I asked you to take me to the doctor, but you forgot. It was the week of one of Julie's big meets. So I made an appointment myself and went over, and got the prescription filled, and put the drops in myself for a week. And *then* it got better."

He looked across the room at me. Even in

the dark, I could see he was upset. But he tried to cover, with this sickening little chuckle. You know — the "no big deal" chuckle. And then he said, "Come on. You're talking like we've neglected you. Haven't we always taken care of you? Made sure you had what you needed?"

I sighed. "Well, of course you haven't let me starve, or go without shoes or anything like that. I don't think the child welfare board is going to come and take me away from you But I don't feel you've given me what I need. When was the last time you actually gave a real thought to me, to what's going on with me, to what I'm interested in? You couldn't even make the end-of-the-year pageant and see me as an icicle."

"Well, you know, honey — your mother and I both work. And when we're not working, well, I thought we all felt Julie's swimming was something we were going to get behind. Even if it meant sacrifices."

"I don't remember agreeing to anything like that. And I *really* don't remember anyone ever asking me how I felt about moving down here, or about spending all our weekends over at Surfcrest, or all our vacation time traveling around to regional meets. I've probably spent more time around pools in my fourteen years than most people do in a lifetime. And —"

He put up his hands, as though I were slugging at him. "I just didn't realize . . . I guess we've got a few communication problems. . . ."

"I think I've been communicating that I want you to pay attention to me and you've been communicating back that you simply don't care."

"Meg," he said softly. "Of course we care about you."

"Do you, Dad?" I said in a quiet voice that cut through the dark silence between us. "Do you *really?*"

"Of course I do. Look, I'm going to go and . . . uh . . . I'm going to talk with your mother." It was what he said whenever he didn't really know what to say. When he was at the door, he turned and said, "Get some sleep. We'll talk more tomorrow."

Get some sleep. Easy for him to say. I was way too upset to even think about sleep. Instead, I went over and kneeled down in front of the window at the end of my attic. I put my arms on the sill and watched the storm, which by now had moved off to somewhere else, and was just vague rumbles and distant popping flashes in the sky.

I thought about the conversation with my dad. I'm not used to talking to my parents so sharply — or to getting away with it. The fact that my dad had let me seemed to say he knew what I was saying was true. Up there, all alone, in the middle of the night, in the top of the house, this somehow seemed like a pretty puny victory. I mean, what difference was it going to make?

Still, when I finally did get back into bed and managed to drift off, I fell into a dream that it was morning and I came outside and my mom and dad were waiting out front, with the car already running and the back seat all fluffed up with pillows for me, and off we went to Disneyworld. It was kind of a fantasy dream, if you know what I mean. I call them "make-right" dreams.

But then, when we finally did get to Disneyworld, it was storming worse than it had in real life. Things had gone way beyond rain, into hailing big, icy stones down on the roof of the car. The noise was so loud it woke me up.

But when I opened my eyes and looked out the window, there was no rain or hail at all. Still, there was definitely a spattering noise against my window screen. I got up and went over and looked down into the yard. It was Joey, tossing handfuls of gravel. I pushed up the window.

"What's up?" I shouted down in the loudest whisper I could manage.

"Big emergency," he whispered back up. "Can you get out?"

I nodded and put a finger over my lips. I held up the fingers of one hand to show him I'd need five minutes.

Meg "Danger Is My Middle Name" Swenson. I was probably going to get in *so* much trouble for this. Grounded until adulthood.

Chapter 18

When I got down to the yard, Joey emerged from behind one of my mother's lemon trees.

"What's the emergency?!" I said in a voice that was a cross between a whisper and a scream.

"Adelaide called. A fishing boat capsized out by the cove. Everyone on board was saved, but the boat was totaled. The oil tanks burst and now there's an oil slick on the waters of the cove. The gulls got caught in it. With oil on their feathers, they can't fly."

"Ohhhh," I said. I just can't stand thinking of little animals or birds getting hurt or in trouble. They seem like such innocent victims.

"So?" Joey said, staring at me expectantly. "Can you help out?"

"Oh, of course."

"I wouldn't hold it against you if you

didn't come. I know you're grounded and I don't want to get you in any more trouble than you already are."

"Oh, Joey, I'm already in so much trouble, this'll just be a couple more drops in the bucket. But what can we do? I mean, how is it we're supposed to help?"

"We've got to try to get them wiped off. I've got a dozen rolls of paper towels in my bike baskets. It was all they had at the 7-Eleven. Adelaide's already out there. She called from a pay phone on the beach road."

"Well, what are we waiting for?" I said and went to the garage to get my bike.

It looked as if we were the first people out after the storm. Everything was pretty crazy-looking. Stop signs were bent, and palm fronds and green coconuts that had worked loose from the trees were lying all over the streets. Bob's Sunoco was now "ob's" Sunoco, with the B lying in a field across the highway.

Outside town, where there were no sewer grates, the roads were still flooded. We just kept riding fast, even when the water was up to the hubs of our bike wheels. In a way, it was as though Joey and I were the last people on earth. Or the first. It was a very close experience, being out there together. We didn't say anything. We kind of didn't have to.

We dropped our bikes at the foot of the dune, split up the rolls of towels, and started the climb. The dunes are always rough going, but this morning with the sand so soggy, the way up was like some kind of Marine boot camp leg test. About three quarters of the way, I gave up, sank to the sand, and told Joey to go on without me.

"I just don't think I can make it," I said.

"Okay," he said. "Just take it easy. Give me your paper towels. I'll save as many gulls as I can. If Adelaide and I can't get to all of them, well. . . ." He stopped and stared off into the distance, then added with a crack in his voice, "Poor little guys."

"Well, wait a minute," I said. "I can probably make it. I think I'm getting my second wind."

I got up and started climbing again. When we'd gone another few yards, I turned and asked Joey, "Hey. Were you guilt-tripping me back there?"

"Sure," he said and grinned. "Worked, didn't it?"

I would've tackled him, but I didn't have the energy.

When we finally got to the top of the dune and looked down, I was instantly glad I'd pushed myself to make it. The gulls really were in trouble. The waters in the cove were black and shiny and opaque — in stark contrast with the clear turquoise of the surrounding sea. The oil lay like an ominous carpet, rolled out from the fishing boat, which was lying on its side a half mile out to sea.

On the beach, Adelaide was rushing around, furiously trying to wipe off as many gulls as she could. But there were too many birds and only one Adelaide. I don't know what would have happened if we hadn't come.

We took a fast roll down the dune, losing the towels twice, and having to climb back to fetch them. When we got to the beach, and saw the problem up close, it was even more pathetic. There must've been about fifty gulls, their formerly white, fluffy feathers slicked down with black oil. They tottered around the beach, bewildered and confused, not understanding why they couldn't take off.

Adelaide looked up from the gull she was wiping at the moment and started to cry, she was so happy that we'd made it there.

"Reinforcements! The cavalry is here!"

Sweetie picked up the mood and barked his happy bark, and did his straight-up, all-four-legs-off-the-ground jump.

I grinned and stood there for a moment, feeling like some big hero. Then I realized

I hadn't done a thing yet, and, more to the point, I didn't even know what *to* do. Adelaide seemed to read my mind.

"Just do one bird at a time," Adelaide said, handing me a box of cornstarch and a bucket of soapy water. "Pick one bird up and sprinkle it with cornstarch to soak up the oil. Then dunk some paper towels in the detergent and gently wipe off as much of the oil as you can."

"Won't they try to get away?" I asked.

"Probably. But without wings, they're pretty easy to catch."

I was doubtful about the whole business, but gave it a try. I bent over a cluster of scurrying birds, reached in, and pulled out my first gull. I'd never held a bird before. It was a pretty amazing sensation. Almost scary. It was so fragile I could feel its little heart going *blip-blip-blip* against the palm of my hand. It was as though its feathers were just this thinnest covering over its life.

I tried to be incredibly gentle, holding it under its little chest, wiping with the flow of its feathers. There was no way to get all the oil off. About the best I could do was get it from pitch-black to dingy gray.

"They look like big-beaked pigeons," I said, surveying the scene after we'd cleaned most of the gulls.

"Don't let *them* hear that," Adelaide

cautioned me. "They feel they're much prettier than pigeons."

I didn't ask how she'd received this information.

The three of us had been working hard for maybe an hour. By the time I stopped to notice, it had gone from dawn to morning. I looked over at Joey. He was down on his knees, wiping off a bunch of baby gulls, picking them up one by one, ever-so-gently, wiping each with a soapy paper towel, then setting the bird back down on the sand, giving it a little push to get it back in the flying spirit again.

Seeing him like this, I felt my heart fill with a new kind of feeling for Joey — different from the kissing feeling, but definitely in the love category. This was turning out to be a strange summer, showing me sides of the people in my life I hadn't suspected were there. Joey turning out to be so sensitive. Julie turning out to have so much more to her than just swimming. I guess I was seeing different sides of myself, too.

When we'd wiped off the last of the gulls, and Adelaide had gone over the far dunes to see if there were any strays stranded up on the next beach, Joey and I just kind of collapsed onto the sand.

"I think we did okay," he said.

"We did great," I corrected him, then looked over at him while he looked out at the ocean. I told him, "I feel like so much has been happening to me lately. And that you keep being part of all these experiences. And I. . . ." I broke off there.

"You what?" Joey said, not about to let me off the hook.

"I'm not sure," I said. "I think maybe I'm falling in like with you."

"In *like?*"

"Well, something that keeps taking me by surprise."

"But it couldn't be love, because I'm not the redheaded guy of your dreams, right?" he said seriously.

I didn't get a chance to answer, though. I looked up and saw that a few of the gulls had decided to try out their wings, unsuccessfully, and were staggering awkwardly across the sand back toward the water.

"Oh, no!" I shouted at them, and jumped to my feet and started trying to wave them away. "Not *that* way, you dopes!"

But they headed right back into the oily water. And so we had to get Adelaide and bring the gulls in and wipe them down all over again.

"I guess that answers today's science question: How smart are gulls?" I said to both of them.

* * *

A few minutes later, there were the sounds of other voices. The three of us looked up. Coming over the top of the dune was a small group of people — a woman dressed in white and two guys carrying some kind of equipment.

"Professional bird washers?" Joey guessed jokingly, but Adelaide, who spent more time out on the streets than me or Joey, knew right off what was going on.

"It's a TV minicam unit," she said, then pulled a pair of beat-up binoculars from her carryall. When she'd gotten a clearer look, she put down the binoculars and told us, "Channel six. We're about to be famous — locally at least."

"Oh, no!" I cried.

"You don't want to be famous?" Adelaide said. "You want to remain an unsung heroine?"

"It's not that, exactly," I admitted. "It's that now I'm sure to get caught violating my grounding. My parents always watch the news on channel six."

Chapter 19

Good thing my parents are late sleepers. When I got back around ten in the morning, they were still in their room, the house still quiet.

I took the longest shower of my life with a bar of this industrial soap I found by my dad's workbench. It has sand or something in it and is supposed to be able to get grime off the hands of auto mechanics. Covered with oil as I was, I used it all over and emerged a bright pink.

And totally exhausted. I couldn't remember ever being more tired. I could barely climb up to the attic and I think I fell asleep as I was crawling into bed. I probably would've slept the whole day through if it hadn't been for the city tree-cutting guys. I guess they were cutting down all the branches broken by the storm and now dangling dangerously. These guys have major power saws and this branch-eating machine that makes a racket no one could possibly sleep through. And so, thanks to them, I was up — if not truly awake — by eleven-thirty.

I came down into the kitchen to find everyone having breakfast. And by everyone, I mean the whole family. And by whole family, I mean my mother, my father, my sister, and the swim coach, Ian Braithwaite.

He was sitting (of course) at the head of the table, dominating the scene with his dark wavy hair and deep tan and booming voice, and six-feet-four presence. Ian just kind of emanated waves of celebrity and power. You got the feeling he ranked himself on the Important Guy list somewhere between Bruce Springsteen and Prince Charles.

"We'll start her off on low-impact workouts," he was saying now, as he spread organic peanut butter on his sprouted wheat English muffin. My parents were focused so intently on him they looked like they were about to take notes. Needless to say, they didn't notice me come in. Julie either, but not because she was so intent on what Ian was saying. Actually, she was looking out the window, at the peonies, distracted. This was really weird. Julie usually acted like Ian was her guru.

"Then we can move her up to full morning workouts, with some free weight work to. . . ." Ian was going on. But my mother had noticed that Julie wasn't paying attention.

"Julie," she said sharply. "Ian's planning your fall schedule here. You're not being very courteous."

Ian stopped in the middle of his sentence, still holding the English muffin aloft, but now looking as though a pesky bee were buzzing around his head, as if he was being bothered to his limit.

All eyes turned to Julie, waiting for her to apologize for drifting off. But when she finally said something, it was far from an apology.

"Uh . . . well . . . the thing is, nobody's asked *me* how I feel about swimming this fall."

"What do you mean?!" my mother said. "How you feel about swimming? You swim. Swimming is what you do. What else *would* you do?"

Julie smiled a little and said, "Well, I thought I might live my life for a while. See how it goes without workouts and training schedules. You know — I thought I'd just punt. Like every other teenager in the world."

"But you're *not* every other teenager in the world," Ian said in this patronizing voice he used on Julie whenever she expressed an idea of her own.

"That's right," my mother swung in, "you're a special girl. You're a world-class athlete in the making."

"Maybe," Julie admitted. "And maybe I'll be a world-class athlete in reality someday. But right now I need to find out who I am *out* of the pool." And when she'd finished saying this, she kept them all at bay — my parents and Ian — by just holding them off with a steady stare of conviction.

"All *right*, Julie!" I burst out. I couldn't help it. She looked over at me and exploded into a laugh.

"Are you saying you want to quit swimming entirely?" my dad finally said, in this ultracalm voice, the kind of voice firemen use to try to talk people back in from the ledges of skyscrapers.

"Maybe she just means for a couple of weeks," my mom said. "After all, she's been cooped up here with that cast on all these weeks. She probably just needs a little burst of freedom before she gets down to business again. Maybe we could all take a little vacation together. To Fort Lauderdale. We could visit the Swimming Hall of Fame."

I had picked up a piece of toast off the counter, and the prospect of this "vacation" made me practically swallow it whole. Ian was also unhappy with this idea, but for different reasons.

"I just wouldn't let this little 'break' get too out-of-hand," he said coolly. "We don't want to lose her momentum. We don't want her to decide to come back to competitive swimming — only to find out it's *too late*."

My parents were clearly intimidated by this casual threat. They both looked jumpy. Julie, though, held her ground and just gave everyone a look that said she wasn't going to be bullied.

"Uh . . ." my mother finally said to Ian, "maybe you'd better let us talk to her . . . alone."

When Ian had huffed out the door, my mother really pinned Julie down.

"Just what's going on here, if I may ask? All of a sudden, you don't want to swim — "

"Not all of a sudden, really," Julie said. "I've been feeling this way for a while."

"Then why didn't you tell us?"

"I don't know," Julie said. "Scared, I guess. That you'd be mad — after all the time you've put in on my swimming. After moving down here and all."

"That's why it's important that you don't stop now," my mother said. "Now that you're so close. We've given over our lives so you could be a world-class athlete."

Then, in a very quiet voice, Julie stopped everything by saying, "Maybe you did it all so you could be the *parents* of a world-class athlete."

This really stung them, especially my mother, who lashed back. "This is really about that punk, that motorcycle boy, isn't it?" she snapped. But Julie just kept her cool.

"No," she said in a voice that dripped icicles. "This is really about *me*. What *I* need. And what I need right now — and maybe for quite a bit longer than two weeks — is for everyone to get off my back and just let me be."

"What's going on here?" my dad said, like he still didn't get it. "Last night Meg blew up at me because she's not getting enough attention from us. Now you tell us we're hassling you with too much."

"But don't you see!" I burst out. "Both things are true!"

"Meg's right," Julie backed me up. "Everything in this family is out of balance. You don't know your own daughters — either of them!"

My parents looked at each other for a long moment, as though they were trying to say things to each other, but couldn't find the starting word.

Finally my mother turned to Julie and

me and said in a voice that sounded more hurt than angry, "In the beginning, the important thing seemed to be to make sure Julie felt like a true member of the family. I guess maybe we went a little overboard, and wound up losing Meg in the process. But really, honey," she said to me, "we've just always felt you were such a secretive kid, off in your own world."

"You just never tried to get inside it," I said. "I don't really have any secrets."

Famous last words. Not half an hour later, when this talk between me and Julie and our parents had wound down to four thoughtful silences, my dad tried to distract us all a bit by turning on the TV.

"Let's see what havoc that storm wreaked. I heard something about a boat capsizing." And with that, he turned on the little black-and-white TV on the kitchen counter and whose face filled the screen? Three guesses.

There I was, with the reporter woman standing next to me with her arm draped over my shoulders as she talked into the camera.

"This is fourteen-year-old Meg Swenson, a real local heroine. At dawn this morning . . ."

"Dawn?!" my mother said.

". . . on the beach at Sea Urchin Cove . . ."

"Sea Urchin Cove?!" my dad said.

"Meg and her friends Joey Moss and Adelaide Higgins . . ."

"Adelaide Higgins?!" Julie said.

". . . saved over fifty gulls grounded by an oil slick created by the capsized fishing boat, the *Esmerelda*. Meg — just how did you find out the gulls were in trouble?"

Mercifully, the telephone picked this particular moment to ring. My dad picked up.

"Yes. Yes she is. Just a moment." He held out the receiver to me and said, "The *Marlin Beach Herald* wishes to speak to Miss Swenson."

I reached for it and asked him, "You're not going to ground me again for this, are you?"

"No," he said grouchily. "I don't want to get a rep around town as the guy who grounded the heroine of the day."

The newspaper wanted to take a photo of me and Joey and Adelaide and, hopefully, a few recuperating gulls. Julie came with me. She was getting so fast on her crutches that she could almost keep pace with a terrifically wimpy person, like myself.

"What do you think?" I asked her when we were on our way over to the cove. She knew what I was talking about.

"I think we just turned their world upside down — then shook it."

"But do you think it's going to make any difference?"

"For sure if I don't go back to swimming, the central thing around there is going to change. We may all have to actually talk to each other!" Then she got more serious. "Whatever happens, it was a good thing — us telling them. Things had gone too far wrong, and they weren't going to get any better all by themselves."

"You were great," I told her.

"You weren't bad yourself," she said and gave me a hug — which, if you're a person on crutches, is quite a trick.

The newspaper was supposed to take our photos in the afternoon at the cove, but Joey was late and so Julie and I just hung out with Adelaide, waiting.

"I think we managed to save every single gull," Adelaide said to me.

"Yeah, and that's great," I said. "The sad part is it looks like we lost our secret cove in the process." I gestured at the small crowd milling about — people who'd come down to see the slick, and to watch the fishing boat, which was about to go under.

But Adelaide just shook her head and gave me a wink and whispered, "No problem."

"What?" I whispered back.

"I know another place. Top secret. And

very hard to get to." She stopped and gave me the eagle eye. "Think you're up to it?"

I laughed a little and told her, "I'll give it a try."

Then this bunch of grade school kids came up wanting autographs from me and Adelaide. Stars for a day. A few kids from my school were in the crowd, too, including Jill Percival and Ron Mussman.

"So, what are you?" he asked me, "Mighty Mouse, come to save the day?" I was beginning to see that although Ron was majorly gorgeous, he had the sense of humor of your average rhinoceros.

Jill giggled at this, though. She would. Then she said to me in her most sickening voice, "Yes, Meg, I'm surprised you have time for good works. I mean doesn't saving birds take you away from your great artistic career?"

I gathered myself up to my fullest height, and put my nose snootily into the air and said, "Funny you should mention that, Jill, but there's going to be a show of my drawings over at the Hubbell Gallery next month. I'll try to remember to send you a special invitation."

As far as I'm concerned, life doesn't give a person these kind of moments often enough.

* * *

And then something in the distance caught my attention — someone coming up over the top of the dune. You could spot him a mile away. He had the reddest hair I'd ever seen on a person. At first I thought maybe it was the guy of my dreams. But then, when he started rolling down the dune, I knew who it was. Nobody rolled quite like that except Joey.

He came walking up to me, oblivious to all the people on the beach.

"So?" he said when he was standing right in front of me. "What do you think?"

"How could you?" I sputtered.

"Easy. You just get a kit at the drugstore. This color's called Flame. Do you think I should've gone for something more subtle? They had Autumn Russet."

"I mean . . ." I sputtered again.

"Come on," he said, walking me off down the beach a ways, so we could have a little privacy. "I just want the chance to be the guy of your dreams."

Even though it was a pretty wonderful moment, it was also a pretty funny one. I mean, you had to *see* his hair. It was impossible not to laugh, which got him laughing, too. And then we started hugging each other.

"Oh, Joey," I told him. "This has been such a *strange* week. . . ." And then every-

thing just sort of came tumbling out —
about Jenkins and the gallery show. About
my parents and the big scene with them
and my hopes for some changes around our
house. And somewhere in the middle of this
rush, I realized that telling Joey stuff had
become such a big part of my life. And
maybe that meant something — something
I hadn't thought of before. And so I told
him about that, too. "Not to mention that
I really do . . . enjoy kissing you," I said,
teasing him, dancing around and away
from him on the sand. But I didn't dance
quite fast enough and he caught me and
spun me into a pretty amazingly wonderful
kiss for it being broad daylight on a
crowded beach. Luckily, we were fast
enough to put our hands in front of our
faces as the newspaper camera started
clicking away.